KYLE

Riding Hard, Book 6

JENNIFER ASHLEY

JA/AG Publishing

Chapter One

✧❦✧

K yle knew from second number three he wouldn't survive this ride. The bull twisted like a demon, Kyle's hand slipped, and the crowd groaned.

He and the bull went up in the air, hung for a long moment, and descended, the animal's legs hitting the earth like piledrivers. Kyle's body jolted, his teeth clacking, the strap burning through his glove.

Waves of noise poured from the crowd. Half the county wanted to see him on his ass, and half wanted him to win, to be their champion. The ride would give Kyle enough points toward this year's finals, another belt to hang in his trophy room.

But determination, guts, and the prospect of the win were no substitute for a good grip, no defense against a bull that had been bred in hell.

Kyle put aside his ego and looked for a soft place to land.

He made it to 5.318 seconds before he was airborne. The bull spun in place, and Kyle saw its gigantic horns waiting to gouge him when he came down.

There was a flash of fiery red hair and dead-white faces as a pair of rodeo clowns dashed from the rail to chase the bull out of Kyle's path.

Kyle tried to roll with the fall, tucking in for the landing, but the ground rushed up too fast. He hit the dirt—hard—and heard the crack of ribs.

The bull broke evaded the clowns in the ring and lumbered back to Kyle, rage in every stride.

He had to get up off his ass, but his legs weren't working. Shit, had he busted a knee? An ankle? Not his foot, he hoped fervently. Foot bones were a bitch to heal and having to ask his brother to help him walk would rankle.

Kyle seriously couldn't get up. The only thing worse than taking a bad fall and hobbling away was being tossed out of the ring by the bull. He'd seen it happen, and it looked like it could happen to him today.

At the last second, the burlier of the two clowns jumped in front of the bull then ran like hell when the bull focused on him. Kyle's vision blurred as the second clown trotted to him and leaned down to peer at him.

Kyle blinked as he took in butter-yellow hair under the wild red wig and sky-blue eyes in a worried face. The white and red clown makeup couldn't disguise the sweet curve of her cheek, just like the plaid shirt and jeans didn't hide her compact, shapely body.

What the fuck?

"Anna ..." Kyle tried to say, but the word was a croak.

Anna Lawler, Riverbend's large animal vet—Dr. Anna as she was fondly called—put a surprisingly strong hand on his shoulder. "Hold still."

"Are you shitting me?" His voice was cracked, breathy.

"What the hell are you doing in here? That's one crazy bull. Get the hell out."

Anna ignored him. She ran small but competent hands down Kyle's arms and over his ribcage—Kyle groaned—and down his belly to his thighs.

"Damn, darlin'. Wait 'til we're in private."

Anna didn't bother to tell him to shut up. She probed all the way down his thighs, pushing at his kneecaps then down his shins to his ankles. No stabbing pain, thank God.

The bull swept by, driven into the pen beyond the chute by the burly clown and a couple more who'd joined the chase. Only Kyle and Anna remained in the ring with the crowd clapping and stomping as they chanted his name, waiting to see whether he lived or died.

Anna did the same test on his arms and gloved hands before she beckoned to the burly clown who'd jogged back in. Hal Jenkins was a brute of a man, his face barely softened by the rosy cheeks and paint outlining his mouth. A former bull rider who'd given it up after one too many falls, Hal was a good wrangler and tough as an ox.

Hal wrapped an arm around Kyle's shoulders and hauled him up. Anna was on Kyle's other side, bracing him as he found his balance.

Anna was a nice bundle under his arm, her hair smelling of flowers instead of dirt and cow shit. The scent cut through Kyle's pain, made him want to sink into her, tell Jenkins to lose himself, flow down into the warm scent of Anna Lawler.

Where she'd rip him a new one. Anna was by no means a sweet, gentle soul—except with animals. They loved her.

Kyle steadied himself, letting go of his rescuers to show he was okay. He waved at the crowd, and they cheered.

His biggest fans, the clump of women with T-shirts

bearing his name or slogans like "Bull Riders Do It Harder," called to him, asking if he was badly hurt. Could they kiss it better? And more suggestive remedies.

Aware of Anna's belligerent scowl, Kyle waved once more. He blew one or two kisses at the ladies and then let Jenkins and Anna guide him, pain kicking his ass now, out of the ring.

A COUPLE OF BUSTED RIBS AND A LOT OF PULLED MUSCLES meant the season was over for Kyle.

He'd been injured before from falling off bulls, and a couple of times from rock climbing, but never this far into a great year. He'd been in the lead, had already landed a couple of nice money prizes, and had a fine chance at the grand championship. Sponsors had been sniffing around, anxious for Kyle Malory to endorse their products—the money they were talking about was substantial. So, of course, he'd had to draw the nastiest bull on the circuit and knock himself out of the running.

As he hunkered down at home to recover, Kyle came to understand what "fair-weather friends" meant. By three weeks into his recovery—pain meds, doctor appointments, and physical therapy—pretty much everyone had deserted him.

During his few days in the hospital, a handful of the buckle bunnies had come to cheer him up. He hadn't been able to drink the beer they'd brought him, but that was okay —they downed plenty of it themselves and crawled all over him when the nurses' backs were turned. He'd had to tell them to go when their enthusiasm kept jabbing his ribs, which hurt like hell. His libido had backed way off, hiding in a corner, while pain won first place.

Once Kyle was home, and it was clear he wasn't coming out of his house for a while, his supporters dropped away one by one. The sponsors wanted a bull rider who could actually ride and win. The ladies wanted a guy they could parade around to their friends and who wasn't too sore to do the deed.

The guy groupies who followed his career—and yeah, some wanted to sleep with him too—found another rider to cheer for. Even Kyle's closest friends started to have other things to do than visit an increasingly morose dude who could barely walk from his bed to the bathroom.

After a while, the only people Kyle saw were his brother and youngest sister. His second sister, Lucy, had high-tailed it back to her life in Houston once she'd realized Kyle was going to live. She had a squillionaire boss boyfriend who doted on her, and Kyle couldn't blame her for bailing. Even his mom went home to Austin, although Kyle had to more or less shovel her out the door. Kyle was out of danger, but now the healing had to commence.

That left Ray, who was busy running the ranch and doing his own thing, and baby sister Grace, who had a husband and family on the other side of town and couldn't devote much time to her favorite brother anymore.

Which meant that most of the days and some of the nights, Kyle was completely alone.

Healing sucked.

Kyle sat at the window of his bedroom on one of his alone days, wishing his pain meds would let him have a beer. The meds made his world a little hazy, but it wasn't the same as a beer buzz. Beer buzzes came with friends, pool games, talking about whatever, and getting laid. Meds just made him queasy.

The business of the ranch rolled on below. Ray and Kyle trained cutting horses and raised a few of their own. They usually ran a small herd of cattle, fifty head at most. Ranching ate time, and Ray was doing a lot of Kyle's grunt work now.

Kyle could still answer the phone and dink with the computer, but most of that was left to a secretary down in the office. She wasn't a cute fluffball of a secretary in a tight sweater by any means. Margaret was fifty-two, sun-bronzed and wiry from her years of riding and roping, and she didn't take shit from anyone. She also knew a lot about running a ranch, having worked for the Malorys for years. Kyle kept out of her way.

The only refreshing note in the tedium of his days was Anna.

Not that she came to visit Kyle or even to ask if he was all right. Her visits were purely professional, about the horses and cattle. With as many animals as the Malorys had, one was always getting sick, so Anna was a frequent caller.

Kyle's room overlooked a sweep of field that rolled to a cottonwood-lined creek at the end of their property. The land was lush and green, and now in September, the deep blue sky spread its glory above the ranch, a cool breeze creeping in through Kyle's open window.

Below him, Anna, with chaps over her jeans and a leather apron protecting her chest, fired up her portable forge to replace a shoe Ray's favorite horse had thrown.

Kyle watched as Anna guided the blue roan to the hitching post in the open space between house and riding rings, and tied his lead rope in a competent slip knot. She then busied herself around the forge, putting her rasps and tongs within easy reach, filling a vast bucket with water.

She was the most interesting thing Kyle saw out this window, that was for sure. Anna wore her blond hair in one long braid, the end of which touched her belt when she stood up. Her jeans molded to a fantastic ass, and her loose shirt made him imagine all kinds of wonders beneath it.

Anna caressed the roan's fetlock until he raised his foot, happy to rest it in Anna's lap. Horse wasn't stupid. Anna scraped its hoof with her file to even it out and smooth it to take the shoe.

Once that was done, she tested a ready-made shoe against the hoof then grasped the shoe with her tongs and thrust it into the hot forge. When the shoe glowed red, she removed it from the forge, positioned it on her anvil, and bent to tap the shoe into shape.

The best part. Kyle forgot about his pain, his meds, his boredom, his loneliness. He got lost in Anna's shapely ass as she leaned over the shoe, her body moving as she hammered the hot iron.

He never had found out what the hell she'd been doing in the ring when he'd taken his fall. She'd been playing rodeo clown, but why? She could've gotten herself seriously hurt.

Anna plunged the shoe into her bucket of water, the loud hiss reaching Kyle in his room. She tested the cooled iron against the roan's hoof once more and returned to heat and tap the shoe again.

So nice.

When Anna rose to thrust the hot shoe once more into the water, she glanced up and saw Kyle in his window. Her smooth, serene face crumpled into an immediate scowl.

Kyle felt his mouth stretching, and realized he was grinning like a fool. But hell, he was on meds, and she was the best thing he'd seen in a long time.

A slow flush reddened Anna's face as she realized she'd been pointing her butt toward his window. "Enjoying the view?" she called up to him.

Kyle's grin widened. "I sure am."

Anna glared. "Back off, Kyle. I'm trying to do my job."

"Go ahead. I don't mind."

"Well, I *do*. Get out of that window and stop staring at me."

Kyle gave her a lazy salute. "Yes, ma'am."

He'd leave the window if that made her feel better. In fact, he was motivated to heave himself to his feet, grab the cane his doctor insisted on, and hobble from his room, down the stairs, and outside to the porch.

Chapter Two

K yle shuffled down the porch steps and halted at the bottom, putting his hand on the post to steady himself. This was as far as he was going for now.

He watched Anna test the shoe once more against the roan's hoof then return to her forge to heat it again and set it on the anvil. Her hammer landed precisely on the metal and quickly made it do what she wanted.

"You're pretty damn good at that," Kyle remarked.

Anna jerked up. "Shit. *Kyle.*"

"Hey, you told me to get out of the window. It's way up there." Kyle pointed to the bedroom he'd spent too much time in, and not in a fun way.

Anna looked wild about the eyes. "Sneaking up on me isn't any better."

"Just coming down to be hospitable. Want anything? Cold water?"

"I'm fine." Anna returned to banging at the shoe.

She carried it back to the roan, who waited patiently, his

unshod hoof just touching the ground. Anna patted him. "Good boy."

She easily lifted his hoof, set the shoe, and took nails from her apron pocket, tapping them in. She ran her fingers around the finished shoe and lowered the roan's foot, patting him again.

"What a sweetie you are," she crooned. The horse leaned into her, soaking it up.

"Why are you so nice to him, when to me you're all prickly?" Kyle leaned heavily on his stick, wishing he could rush to her side, help her put away her tools, lead the horse back to the barn for her.

Anna turned to him, the fond look she'd given the horse vanishing. "Cause he's nicer than most guys I know. Patient, not demanding, stands still when I'm talking to him."

Kyle tried a laugh. "Why don't you marry him? Sounds like you'll be perfect together."

Anna gave him a withering look but changed the subject. "Why did you call him Bootsie?" She stroked the horse's neck. "Not a name I associate with two cowboys like you and Ray."

"We didn't. Grace named him. She was about eleven when he was born. Said he looked like he was wearing black knee-high boots." Kyle gestured at the roan's lower legs, which were coal black.

Anna gave him a frown, as though displeased she hadn't been able to embarrass him. What was it with her? She started placing her tools into her box—not throwing them in, because that might startle Bootsie.

Kyle stumped to her. "Let me get that. Put Bootsie away and I'll give you some water on the porch. Or iced tea. Grace might have left a pitcher for me. It's hot today, if you hadn't noticed."

The Valkyrie glare came back. She'd make a good Viking maiden in one of those operas.

"I'm working." She snatched up each tool and shoved it into its precise slot in her toolbox, which was far neater than any toolbox should be.

"You can't take a break? When's your next appointment?"

"None of your business." Anna swung to the forge and slammed dials and banged buttons to shut it down.

This is what he got for trying to be nice. "What are you mad at me about?" Kyle asked, out of patience. "Falling off a bull? Or dancing with you at Ross's wedding?"

Nail on the head. Anna went brick red and turned her back. Fine—Kyle could admire her ass again.

"You know how I feel about bull riding," she muttered. "I'm on the bull's side. If you had a bad fall, it's your own fault for climbing up on his back in the first place."

"Agreed. Then you're pissed off about the dance. You could have said no."

"Not when you were pushing me into it." Anna dragged fallen wisps of hair from her face and pinned her scowl on the forge, which was taking its time cooling down.

Kyle thought back to the night when the Campbell family came together to celebrate Ross and Callie tying the knot. He'd seen Anna watching him, graceful foot tapping to the music. If anyone had been pushy that night, it had been Ray, urging Kyle to ask her out to the floor.

"I remember, I said, 'Hey, Anna. Wanna maybe dance?' And you said, 'Sure, okay.' Like you'd been hoping for a better offer but decided to put up with me."

Anna's mouth tightened. "I don't remember being that rude."

"You're always rude to me. I don't know what I did to you in a former life, but it's getting irritating."

"Well then." Anna closed up the forge, which Kyle assumed was cooled down to safety levels. She untied her apron and then the chaps, folding them up together. "If we don't talk to each other, we'll be all right."

"Was it that bad a dance? I don't think I'm the world's most fabulous two-stepper, but no one's ever complained before."

Kyle recalled the softness of Anna against him as they'd bumped together on the crowded floor, the easy way she'd moved with the music, the soft scent of her perfume, the light touch of her hand. He went warm all over, the sun suddenly burning.

"No, it was fine." Anna said it like a person wanting to get something dire over with, like a shot at the doctor's.

Kyle hid his hurt. "Good. Then put the horse away and get your ass to the porch and have some iced tea. Will it kill you?"

"Probably." Anna marched to Bootsie, freed him with one flick of the halter rope, and led him away.

Bootsie swished his black tail as though flipping Kyle off. Anna glanced over her shoulder at him, and Kyle wouldn't have been a bit surprised if she'd raised her finger at him as well.

———

ANNA MADE SURE BOOTSIE WAS SECURE IN HIS PEN AND THAT

the shoe was solid before making her way back to her forge. He really was a sweet horse.

Kyle, on the other hand ...

The Malory brothers were all Anna disliked in men— overly confident, sure the world owed them for being big, bad dudes, certain all women wanted to jump into bed with them.

And damn it, the women did. Plenty of ladies hung on the rails at the rodeos to watch Kyle, half falling out of T-shirts with his logo on them. They followed him from rodeo to rodeo, to the bar when he was in Riverbend, to the diner, to the feed store. They'd do anything for one look, one touch. They had no shame at all.

She'd been certain that his convalescence would involve a score of buckle bunnies in his room, and was surprised when Grace told her he hadn't had many visitors. Grace had said, with a laugh, that she was sure Kyle being without female company would kill him.

So if Anna despised those women, why was she walking back to the porch where Kyle waited in the shade instead of loading up her forge and driving away?

Anna stiffly climbed the steps and sank into a wicker chair, facing Kyle, who sat four feet away. He pushed a clinking glass of iced tea to her, droplets of condensation clinging to its sides.

"Thank you," she said.

And why, *why*, did her insides turn to jelly as soon as Kyle looked at her with those warm green eyes, truly *looked* at her?

She was sure her tongue had just fallen out of her mouth so she jammed the glass against her lips and took a gulp.

And choked. Anna fought for breath, the tea slipping from her hands.

Kyle caught the glass without spilling a drop and set it down, and then his big hands were on her back.

"You okay?" Kyle's body heat flowed over Anna as he gave her several firm thumps. She coughed, and her windpipe cleared.

"Fine," she gasped.

"You sure?"

Kyle remained at her side, enclosing her in his personal space, concern in his eyes.

"Yes, yes." Anna pushed from him, landing hard against the back of her chair.

Kyle still hovered. "If you're sure."

"I swallowed the wrong way, that's all. No need for you to hurt yourself. Or to grope me."

Kyle's concern vanished. "I wasn't *groping* you." He limped to his chair and lowered himself gingerly. "I was nowhere near your boobs. Or your ass. I was trying to be gentleman-ly." His lips twitched. "Course, I remember when you helped me out of the ring. Your hand was definitely on *my* ass."

Anna's face went hotter than ever. "It was not. Don't flatter yourself."

He grinned, his smile like a heatwave. "It's okay. I didn't mind."

"And you wonder why I'm always 'prickly' with you." Anna jerked her fingers in air quotes. "You make it hard to be nice."

"Do I? I thought I was a sweetheart. Ray's the mean one."

"Ray is always polite to me."

"And I'm not?" Kyle took a long sip of tea, let out a sigh and sat back, the wicker of his chair creaking. "Man, I'll be glad when I'm off meds and can have a beer. Not that Grace doesn't make a mean iced tea." He drank another swallow, and then his razor focus returned to her. "I *am* polite to you. I asked you to dance at the wedding when you were sitting by yourself. I tell you that you look great. I give you a cold drink on a hot day. What more do you want?"

"A little respect."

"Sorry, I didn't realize you were Aretha Franklin. My apologies." He lifted his glass in salute. "I do respect you. You can make a horse stand still while you're nailing metal to its feet. You wrestle a steer into submission easier than cowhands three times your size. I have a lot of respect for you, Anna." He raised his glass again. "But I'm not gonna sing."

Anna sipped her tea. It really was good—she tasted rose petals and a hint of sweetness.

The soothing liquid let her regain her composure. "I didn't see that respect when you were ogling my back end while I was shoeing Bootsie."

Color pushed aside the pallor in Kyle's cheeks. "But it's such a gorgeous back end. Can't you be competent and pretty at the same time?"

She shook her head. "You should hang a sign around your neck. *Warning: So Not PC.*"

Kyle looked perplexed. "Why can't I think a woman has a nice ass? Doesn't mean I'm doing anything about it—not following her home or pinching her or anything weird and creepy like that. I'm just admiring. From afar." He lifted his hands as though showing how much distance lay between the two of them.

"Women weren't made to stand around for you to admire." Anna tried to say it with conviction, but the image of his tight-shirted groupies flashed to her. They certainly wanted Kyle's attention.

"Aw, come on. You can't tell me you don't stare at any guy's ass. Or his abs or his pecs, or whatever women look at. Seriously—tell me straight up you never do. Ever."

Anna's face heated. She opened her mouth to hotly deny it, but with Kyle sitting so near, his body one of the best examples of the male form she'd ever seen, she couldn't speak. She had difficulty lying, so she mostly shut up.

Kyle started to laugh. "See? You ogle men as much as I ogle women. So we're even."

Anna went hotter. "No, we are not. Men are far more threatening to women than women are to men."

Kyle's laughter died in a grimace of pain, and he pressed his hand to his ribs. "Honey, every guy around here knows you turn bulls into steers with a few jabs and a snip. They cross their legs when they see you coming, especially when you're carrying your nippers. I'd say you were definitely a threat to every man in Riverbend."

"I mean in general." Anna waved away a fly. "Women are uncomfortable with men leering at them."

"Who's leering? How dumbass would I look with a leer pasted on my face all the damn time?" He tried one. "Ow. That hurts my cheekbones."

Kyle's distorted face made Anna want to laugh. She stifled the urge with difficulty. "Yeah, but you *notice*. And you don't hide it."

"What is wrong with me telling a woman she looks pretty? Which you do." Kyle skimmed his gaze up and down her. "Seriously. I mean it as a compliment."

"You shouldn't even say *that*."

"You mean I can't even say, with a straight face, my eyes on the ceiling, 'Hello, you look nice today'?" When Anna shook her head, Kyle took on a heavy scowl. "All right, then you're tired and cranky and there's horse shit in your hair."

Anna's hand flew to her head. "Is there?"

Kyle took up a paper towel he'd brought out with the teas, climbed heavily to his feet, and reached with it toward her. "Right there ..."

He touched her head, his hand all kinds of warm. Anna snatched the towel from him and jammed it to her hair, dabbing anxiously.

Kyle sat down with a thump. "What do you want me to do, Anna? Stand ten feet away from you in a straightjacket with duct tape on my mouth? Maybe a blindfold?"

Anna pretended to perk up. "That would be nice."

"Hell." Kyle stood up again with a grunt of pain. "I am so done with this stupid conversation. See you around. Have a good life."

He started for the door, but stumbled, grimacing as he struggled for balance. Anna jumped up to steady him. Her hand landed on his arm, which held steel strength.

"You all right?" she asked softly.

Kyle's eyes were clouded as he looked down at her. "See? You can't keep your hands off me."

Anna didn't let go. "You're hurt. It's different."

"Sure thing, sweetheart. Whatever lets you sleep at night." His face twisted. "Damn, I landed hard off that bull. And don't even say I shouldn't have been on top of him in the first place. I already know that."

Anna opened the door and kept a supporting hold on Kyle as they stepped over the threshold. They entered the kitchen, a large sunny room with a gleaming tile floor, a table in a bay window, and an old-fashioned hutch with antique plates. Modern cabinets and appliances rounded out the room.

This was a bachelor's house these days, but it was pristine. Anna knew the brothers had cleaners come in, plus Grace lived only a few miles away.

The Malorys were a close family, and Anna had always viewed them with envy. She didn't mind being alone much of the time—her folks had moved to Houston while she'd been in college—but sometimes watching Kyle's family gave her a wistful feeling. She'd grown up in Riverbend, had gone to school with Kyle, though Anna hadn't spoken a word to him. She'd been way too shy, and Kyle had never noticed her. She'd been the introverted Lawler girl with gangly limbs who never looked anyone in the eye.

She'd gained more confidence eventually, first when Callie Jones, one of the most popular girls in Riverbend, had formed an unlikely friendship with her, and second when she'd started acing all her classes and had colleges begging her to enroll.

Now Anna could stand up straight and talk to people, mostly about her job—small talk was still tricky.

But she wasn't comfortable with Kyle. He had a big, warm laugh and a smile that melted her bones. Anna never knew what to say to him. What conversation could she have with a solidly muscled guy with a lazy smile that said he'd pay slow attention in the bedroom?

The fact that he looked at her at all turned Anna inside out. But she'd never, ever admit that to anyone, least of all Kyle.

She helped Kyle to a padded Windsor bench in the bay window so he could sink down to it. Her arm was tangled in his, and she went down with him.

Thighs and sides touched, the length of his leg along hers. Kyle looked down at her, his eyes quieting, his mouth smoothing out.

What if she kissed him?

Anna jumped. Where the hell had that come from? She studied Kyle's lips, flat and uncompromising at the moment, but which could flick into the widest grin in a heartbeat.

A brush of whiskers darkened his face, enticing her touch. They'd feel pleasantly rough to her mouth, and warm, like the rest of him.

Because the urge to kiss him was so strong, Anna unwound her arm from his in a few quick jerks and surged to her feet.

"You all right now?" she asked.

Kyle made a movement as though he wanted to rise, but pain wouldn't let him. He fixed his eyes on her, and for a second, Anna feared he could read her mind. He *knew* she wanted to kiss him.

She waited for him to mock her, keep teasing that she liked looking at his ass—which she did. Her cheeks heated, and she knew she'd gone bright red. Her unfortunately pale skin made every blush vivid.

Kyle said nothing. He only looked at her with those green eyes that Riverbend High School girls had wilted over. Correction—some girls had wilted, others had followed him and tackled him. Anna had pretended she hadn't cared about him one way or the other.

"I have to go," she babbled. "Appointments."

"Sure." Kyle rested his hands on his knees. Working hands, rough-skinned, hard. They'd brush Anna's flesh like fine sandpaper.

She yanked her gaze from his lap. Through the window

she saw the abandoned iced teas on the porch and a walking stick lying in the grass beyond. "You left your cane."

Anna was halfway across the room by the time she finished the sentence. She ignored Kyle's, "Leave the damned thing," and raced out the door.

She fetched the stick and the teas, carrying all carefully inside. This she could do—tidy up and take care of hurt bull riders. Her tea glass went into the sink; Kyle's she set on a table where he could reach it. She leaned the cane against the bench.

"Want me to call Ray?" she asked.

"What the hell for? Will you stop treating me like an injured puppy?"

Kyle Malory was so far from an injured puppy that Anna couldn't hold back a laugh. She gulped, trying, so it sounded like a gurgle.

"See you, Kyle."

If she made a dash for it, she could get her stuff loaded and herself off his property in five minutes.

"Anna."

Anna made herself stop at the doorway and turn back. Kyle was exactly where she'd left him, his body still, his eyes fixed on her.

"Thank you," he said quietly.

Anna wasn't sure what he was thanking her for—bringing him his cane? Shoeing his horse? Letting him laugh at her?

She returned his nod, mumbled something, and got the hell out.

She had her forge and tools inside the little trailer hitched to her truck in record time. Not letting herself look behind her at the house, Anna slid into the cab, started up, and peeled out.

At the end of the drive, she had to stop and wait for Ray, who was turning in through the gate. The older Malory brother, who looked so much like Kyle, raised his hand in a polite wave. Anna fluttered her fingers at him and surged past him out to the road.

She clutched the wheel as the Malory ranch dropped behind her. Two miles along, Anna pulled off into the grass, set the brake, and banged her head once on the steering wheel.

"Why the hell does he make me so *stupid!*" she screeched.

"Anna? You all right?"

Anna jerked her head up. Grace Malory had stopped her SUV on the quiet road and peered through her rolled-down window at Anna in concern. The SUV pointed toward the ranch—she must be going to look in on Kyle.

"Yes," Anna all but yelled. "Shoeing a horse. Tiring job."

Grace nodded with understanding. "Want to come back to the house for tea or something? I'm taking Kyle a great big cake." She smiled the Malory smile that had snared Carter's heart. "He says he doesn't like the fuss, but he really does."

"No!" Anna made herself soften her voice as Grace sent her a perplexed look. "No, I have more appointments to get to."

Anna didn't, but that was her business. She could not return to the Malory ranch today. Or ... ever.

"All right." Grace's eyes held curiosity, but she nodded. "You have a good day, Anna."

"Thanks, you too," Anna said automatically.

Grace smiled and pulled away. Anna waited until Grace's dust faded around a bend in the road before she laid her head down on her steering wheel and groaned.

"RAY, I THINK YOU'D BETTER CALL DR. ANNA," KYLE SAID A
week later. "I saw Peetie barfing. Better have him checked
out."

Kyle made this demand from the warmth of the back
porch. He'd given up his bedroom, finding the sunshine good
for his injuries. Plus he could be more involved in the
running of the ranch—the guys who worked for them had no
problem coming up to the porch to talk to him.

Ray Malory, a few years older than Kyle, thicker,
stronger, and in Kyle's opinion, grumpier, stared at his
brother from the bottom of the porch steps. "Peetie probably
ate something stupid. He does it all the time. More curiosity
than sense."

The Malory animals had been having bad luck lately. A
horse woke up lame—or so Kyle inferred from what one of
the ranch hands had told him. Another might have had colic
or something worse. A few cows hadn't wanted to stand up
out in the field, and a cat had given birth to seven kittens.
Each time, Kyle had suggested that Dr. Anna be called, just
in case.

"Better safe than sorry," Kyle said now. "Make sure he
wasn't poisoned. Have Margaret call her."

Ray's eyes narrowed. "Why don't you get up off your ass
and call yourself?"

Kyle moved the stick at his side. "Injured. Remember?"

"You're moving a hell of a lot better now. You could haul
yourself to the office and make a few calls. Or do it on your
cell phone from here. Or are you worried about straining
your pinky? You know, when you quirk it drinking all that
iced tea." He mimed.

"You're full of shit." Kyle used the stick to stand up, exaggerating his grunts and groans. "Margaret likes to make phone calls. She likes to tell everyone in Riverbend to do what she wants."

Ray shook his head, busy and on his way someplace else. "Whatever. Just take care of it."

He strode away, back to the barn, his job, his life.

Kyle took out his cell phone, looked at it, put it back into his pocket, and made his slow and painful way the hundred yards from the house to the trailer that was their office.

Peetie met him halfway, his heavy tail thudding into Kyle's thighs. Kyle patted him, knowing there was absolutely nothing wrong with the dog.

He entered the office. Margaret was on the phone bending someone in Riverbend to her will, and Kyle slid to his desk without a word. He wouldn't be calling Anna or asking Margaret to call her. Way too embarrassing.

Kyle was surprised then, when Anna showed up herself not twenty minutes later. She wasn't alone. A little girl with her—Faith Sullivan, Carter's daughter—waved out the window at Kyle, who'd hobbled to the office doorway. Faith hopped out of the truck and turned to help Anna bring out her medical box.

"Hi, Uncle Kyle," the girl sang as Kyle went out to meet them. "I decided I want to be a vet when I grow up." Anna straightened up next to her, blue eyes sweeping Kyle and making the cool breeze suddenly hot.

Chapter Three

"Anna is taking me around and showing me what she does," Faith went on. "It's for school," she added quickly, as though Kyle would worry about her ditching classes on this fine autumn day. Kyle had ditched plenty in his life, so he'd not sit in judgement.

Anna wore her braided hair coiled on her head, Swiss-Miss style, Kyle called it. She'd look great in a dirndl with one of those lace-up bodices. Picturing her breasts pushed up by the lacing, her legs in smooth stockings, made Kyle's blood stir in low places.

He cleared his throat. "Did Margaret call you out here? Peetie was a little sick, but Ray's right. He probably just ate something. He eats anything. And everything."

Peetie danced around Faith, tail going so hard he'd knock the poor kid over. He didn't look sick at all.

Anna stared at Kyle. "No one called. I'm doing my inspection."

Faith looked up from petting the excited Peetie. "It's another thing vets do. Inspect herds for any disease and to make sure if you say they're grass fed, they're really grass fed. Or else she can't sign off on the certificate."

"Yep," Kyle said. "That's why we're all real nice to Anna."

"It's got nothing to do with being nice," Anna said stiffly. "The herd either passes or it doesn't."

Kyle leaned heavily on his stick. "I was joking. I do that."

"Uncle Kyle's a barrel of laughs." Faith sank to her knees so she could hug a delighted Peetie. "I get to call them Uncle Kyle and Uncle Ray now, because my stepmom is their sister."

Anna knew that—the whole town did—but Anna gave Faith a kind smile. "Ready to be my assistant?"

"Sure!" Faith stood up, dusting off her hands. "I have to work, Peetie." She took the clipboard Anna handed her and gave Kyle a concerned look. "You sure Peetie's all right?"

Kyle could feel Anna's eyes hard on him, like she could peel off his skin with her scrutiny.

"Naw, he's fine." Kyle deliberately met Anna's gaze. The second he did, she swiveled her head away, her cheeks pink. "He probably ate a bug."

"We'll check him when we get back from the field," Anna said to Faith. "You never know. Do you spray herbicide and pesticide?" The question was fired at Kyle.

"I guess so. Ask Margaret."

"Well, you shouldn't. Bad for your animals. Ready, Faith?"

Faith, oblivious to the tension, hugged the clipboard, waved at Kyle, and followed Anna as she strode down the hill. They moved toward the pasture where the Malorys' small herd milled, enjoying their day.

"This is Texas," Kyle called after them. "If we don't spray, the insects will carry everything off. The house, the barns, everything."

Faith turned around and grinned at him before she hurried after Anna. Anna kept her back to him, utterly ignoring him.

Kyle knew he should let her walk away, should stump back to the office and get on with work. Ray had a point— Kyle could help run the ranch even if he couldn't climb up on a horse or bull. His competing days were over for this year, but he could rest up and make a comeback next spring.

None of that involved following Anna and Faith down to the pasture to watch Anna scan the cattle for any obviously sick animals or choose arbitrary ones to test for various diseases.

But for some reason, Kyle set his shoulders, gritted his teeth against lingering pain, and hobbled after them.

WHAT IS HIS PROBLEM? ANNA THOUGHT IRRITABLY AS KYLE came to a stop behind Faith who waited beyond the fence. The two watched Anna weave her way around the steers, avoiding cow pats as much as she could. Did he think she couldn't do her job? Worried she couldn't take care of Faith?

He should realize that she wouldn't allow Faith to come all the way into pastures with her. Likewise, any inoculations or blood draws Anna did today, she'd do on her own. She wasn't about to let a small girl near a bad-tempered steer who might kick her for the hell of it.

Part of the reason she'd agreed to be Faith's mentor for the day was to show by example that large animal practice was messy, smelly, and dangerous. Anna also wanted Faith to understand that in spite of this, a woman could do it. But she wouldn't sugar-coat it. Anna had made her choice, and Faith should be allowed to make hers.

Why Kyle was making it his business, she didn't know.

At least he kept quiet while Anna did her inspection, drew blood, and patted hairy shoulders. Steers never gave her any trouble. They might watch her warily when she approached, but soon they more or less accepted her as another, if odd-looking, member of the herd.

Anna tucked her samples into her case and walked back to the fence where Kyle and Faith waited. There was no way to avoid manure out here, so Anna spent a few moments scraping her boots on the grass before handing Faith her case and climbing over the fence.

"You're good at keeping your cool," Kyle said. "I've got ranch hands afraid to walk in that pasture. They'll go in on horseback, but they get nervous around the cattle."

Anna shrugged as she showed Faith what to mark on the inspection notes. "The steers don't see me as a threat. They also know I'm vegetarian."

Faith laughed. "How do they know that?"

Anna kept a straight face. "I tell them."

The corners of Kyle's mouth twitched, but he didn't crack a smile. "Vegetarian? Darlin', don't preach to a rancher about not eating meat. We have to make a living."

Anna gave him a surprised look. "I don't expect everyone to give up meat. Just me. I can't eat what I've been looking in the eye and having a conversation with. Especially if I helped them be born."

"Aw," Faith said. "That's a good point. I guess I won't eat meat either."

"Okay," Kyle said. "No burgers for you. Or Grant's fantastic chili."

"Well." Faith pursed her lips. "I'll think about it."

Anna hid her amusement by looking through her check-list. Kyle leaned on the post next to her.

"You know, Faith, if you follow Anna around long enough, you'll learn she's against everything we do—eating burgers, training cutting horses, riding bulls."

Seriously, what was he doing? Trying to make her look like a complete stick-up-her-ass?

"Cutting horses get injured," Anna said, trying to sound reasonable. "The quick turns are hard on their legs. They pull tendons and break bones. And you know the cruelty to bulls that goes on."

Faith looked interested, but Anna didn't want to elaborate. People used all kinds of prods, electronic and otherwise, to make the bulls rocket out of the chute. Plus, animals got injured in many ways, some injuries leading to death. She'd put down more than one calf or bull at a rodeo who'd otherwise expire in pain.

"There are incidents," Kyle admitted. "I know that. Me and Ray don't ride in rodeos that shock the bulls or pack the cattle like sardines in the pens and transports. We're not completely oblivious of crap that goes on. But it's not a slaughterhouse. Animals are injured, and people too, yeah." He lifted his walking stick. "But a small percentage."

"Even a small percentage is too much for me," Anna said.

"Animal cruelty goes on everywhere. You can't save them all. Unfortunately."

"But I can save the ones I can." Anna looked Kyle up and down, a handsome cowboy with one elbow on the fence post, sun dappling his face as he pushed back his hat. "Anyway, look at you. You could have killed yourself falling off that bull."

"I know." Kyle gave her a slow nod. "But I didn't."

"Absolutely insane." Anna knew she should stop talking before Kyle snarled at her and trudged away, but her tongue wouldn't cease. "Sitting on a bull who's already angry and stressed and then seeing how long you can hang on when he rightly tries to buck you off is crazy. And *you* win prizes for this."

Kyle's mouth thinned. "It's a little harder than it looks, sweetheart."

"I'd never do it." Faith wrinkled her nose. "I'd fall the instant we were out of the chute."

Anna sent her a grin. "Those bulls wouldn't buck *you*, Faith. They'd know what a sweet thing you are and stand still. They buck off Kyle because they don't like him."

Faith laughed, as Anna had meant her to. "Kyle's pretty good, though," Faith said. "I've been watching him at rodeos all my life. The bulls get points too. There's a champion bull at the end of the season—the best one at jumping and twisting and throwing off riders."

"I'm sure the bull is very proud." Anna returned to checking her sheet, mostly to avoid looking at Kyle.

"People who knock bull riding have never done it," Kyle said with a growl. "I train most of the year and ride in a hell of a lot of rodeos. There's more to it than hanging on to a strap. A little more strenuous than staring at a bunch of steers and writing things on a piece of paper."

"Seriously?" Anna threw aside avoiding Kyle's gaze and glared right into his green eyes. "I went four years to one of the best vet schools in the country. I had to be at the top of my classes in pre-vet just to fill out an application to get in. I worked my ass off and got my D.V.M, but then I had to pretty much beg for work because what large-animal practice wants to hire a woman who's barely five feet tall? Don't even think about comparing riding a bull to years and years of studying and testing and putting up with shit jobs until I proved myself."

Anna ran out of breath, her chest heaving as she tried to catch it. Kyle only stared at her, not looking one bit ashamed.

"I'll give you being smart and all your schooling," he said. "I sucked at school, and you know it. But ranching is tough work, and bull riding is a skill. Just like doctoring animals is a skill. Can we agree on that?"

Anna knew she should shut up. But something drove her on. Maybe it was the way Kyle looked at her, drying up her mouth and tightening her throat. Maybe it was the way she flashed hot every time he spoke, her heart pounding with each movement of his mouth, the way she couldn't keep her gaze from his lips as he took a step closer.

"No, we can't agree," she said, her voice hoarse. "Performing lung surgery on a horse is a hell of a lot trickier than straddling a bull for a few seconds and then falling on your butt."

Kyle halted a mere two feet from her. He pulled down his hat, its brim reaching for her as he stooped to her.

"If bull riding is so damn easy, why don't you try it? Do it —*then* you tell me what's hard and what's easy."

"Don't be stupid. You know I think bull riding is tough on the bull. I will never do that."

"Uh huh. What I hear is you weaseling your way out of it. Tell you what—I'll put you on top of a tame bull. No harnesses, no straps, not one piece of rope on him. I'll even ask him nicely if you can ride him. Then you'll see how hard it is."

Anna was already shaking her head. "No way. You'd

smack him or something to get him to buck. I'm not letting you do that."

Kyle raised his hands. "Promise, no one will touch him."

"No," Anna nearly yelled. "It's a stupid idea. I'm not riding a bull!"

"What about a mechanical one?" Faith asked, and Anna jumped. "Like at that place—Dino's. On the way to Fredericksburg."

Anna did *not* like the way Kyle's lips curved into a sudden smile. "Faith, you're a genius. I can't see Anna calling the humane society about how Dino's treats a piece of machinery."

Panic formed a cold bubble in Anna's stomach. "It's still dangerous. People get hurt on those."

"I've seen plenty of women ride Dino's bull, and ride it well," Kyle said. "What's the matter, Anna? Afraid you'd have to eat your words? Admit it's not so easy?"

"No," Anna snapped. The panic kept welling, but the light in Kyle's eyes would not let her back down. He'd laugh, he'd crow, he'd never let her hear the end of it. "I'm not afraid. Figuring out how to balance on a machine is still miles easier than being a vet."

Kyle's grin widened. "So you'll do it?"

"Yes," Anna heard herself say. "I will."

"Yay!" Faith did a fist-pump.

"Sweet." Kyle's face was hard but triumph waited behind it. "How about we make this even more interesting?"

They seemed to be closer now. Sunshine burnished the dark whiskers on his jaw, where Anna had wanted to run her hand the last time she'd seen him.

"You mean a bet?" she asked nervously. "I don't want to take your money."

"Oh, not for money, honey."

Anna's heart beat thick and fast at his hot grin. "If you're going to suggest something disgusting, remember Faith is standing right here. Don't make me have to punch you."

Kyle sent her an incredulous look. "What kind of asshole do you think I am? Keep your mind out of the gutter, Doctor. If you can't stay on that mechanical bull for ten seconds, then you agree to go on a date with me."

Anna's knees went weak. A date with Kyle Malory? Walking into a restaurant on his arm, having him hold out her chair. He brushing the small of her back, asking in his low rumble what she'd like to order. Walking her to her doorstep afterward, where he'd lean to softly kiss her ...

The heady fantasy dissolved to show Kyle in front of her, a wicked gleam in his eyes. With Kyle, he might mean a hot dog at a movie followed by unvarnished sex. Which would be sweaty, raw, crazy, wild ... and amazing.

Anna felt the blush come hard, and saw Kyle's answering glee. Damn it, why couldn't she control her face around him?

"What kind of date?" she managed to ask.

"The best kind. A dinner at Chez Orleans. I'll pick you up in a fancy car, bring you flowers, chocolates, whatever you want."

Anna's brows shot high. "Chez Orleans?" It was the most expensive restaurant in River County with exquisite food prepared by a Cordon Bleu-trained man who'd tired of the frenzied life of a celebrity chef. He'd moved from New York City to White Fork to relax and cook what he wanted. "Will they let you in, in your cowboy boots?"

"I'll wear a suit. I *have* heard of them. How about it? You stay on that bull, I'll give you a night on the town. Well, a night at a nice restaurant in White Fork."

Anna rubbed her chin as though pondering. "That's if *you* win. What do I get if *I* win?"

Kyle's grin returned. "If you can hang on for ten seconds, I'll concede you're right, that bull riding is too easy."

"Oh, I'd want a little more than that."

Faith broke in. "I have a great idea. How about, if you lose, Uncle Kyle, you follow Anna around when she works and do all the grunt work for her, like opening gates, catching steers, picking up feces samples …"

Anna's face cooled as she imagined the smug Kyle having to scrabble in a muddy farmyard full of ooze for a good fecal sample, or to hold a bottle for a urine sample, or even better, a semen one. Her smile blossomed.

"All right. It's a bet."

"Awesome." Kyle seized the hand she stuck out and shook it hard.

He had a firm grip, callused fingers, and so much warmth. Anna looked into his eyes, green like dark jade, and had the feeling she'd just made a big, big mistake.

KYLE ARRIVED AT DINO'S WITH SECONDS TO SPARE. HE HADN'T been cleared for driving yet, so he'd had to rely on Ray for transportation. Ray had been late getting back to the ranch from wherever, and Kyle seethed with impatience the whole drive.

Ray had been disappearing from the ranch for long stretches of the day, which wasn't like him. Kyle believed in giving his big brother his own space, but Ray had been more close-mouthed than usual.

"Margaret was looking for you earlier," Kyle mentioned

as they rode away from the few lights of Riverbend. "Couldn't even get you on your phone."

He left it there. Up to Ray to answer, or not.

Ray shot him a glance, his eyes glittering in the darkness before he returned his gaze to the road. "Sorry. Busy."

That was cryptic, even for Ray. But Kyle had his own problems—he'd pry things out of Ray later.

Dino's was an old-fashioned cowboy bar between Fredericksburg and Johnson City that catered to tourists who were looking for a bit of the Old West. It had sawdust on the floor and cowboy hats on the wall, country music on the speakers, steaks on the grill, and a mechanical bull in a big room in back.

Real cowboys came here anyway because Riverbend didn't have many places to go out for the night. There was Mrs. Ward's diner and Sam's bar, and Chez Orleans if you wanted to spend the big bucks. That was about it. So Riverbenders headed to Dino's for chili, steak, two-stepping, local bands, and the bull.

Anna had agreed to meet them there at eight-thirty on this Saturday night. At eight-twenty-nine, when Kyle walked in, the place was packed. Kyle's heart sank—shy Anna was uncomfortable around too many people. Not only might she refuse to go through with the ride, but she might think Kyle was trying to humiliate her.

Not his intention at all. Kyle wanted to prove a point, not embarrass her. He didn't want her mad at him for this too.

Anna was already there, Kyle saw as he and Ray pushed through the crowd. She turned angry blue eyes to Kyle.

Kyle saw the reason for her anger in the next second. All of Riverbend had come, it looked like, and all were talking excitedly about the bet.

"She's gonna hand you your ass, Malory!" was the gist of the comments heading his way.

The entire Campbell clan was present, from Adam to Ross along with their wives, which included Kyle's youngest sister, Grace. They'd brought the kids too, at least the ones who could walk—Faith; Dominic, Tyler's stepson; and Manny, the lanky teen Ross mentored.

All were avidly interested in why Kyle had challenged Anna to ride the mechanical bull in Dino's back room.

Chapter Four

"Faith," Kyle growled, bending a stern eye on the girl. "You sure spread the word."

Faith looked back in all innocence. She did the guiltless expression well, in spite of being Carter's daughter—Carter had been in shitloads of trouble as a kid. Or maybe that's who she'd learned it from.

Faith stuck her hands in her pockets and grinned impudently at Kyle. "You and Anna didn't say I couldn't tell anyone."

No, they hadn't. When Kyle and Anna had sealed the bet, Kyle had been fixed on Anna's soft hand in his, her eyes as blue as the bluebonnets that covered the Hill Country in spring.

He'd been busy waxing poetic in his head and forgot that an eleven-year-old of one of the biggest families in town watched eagerly.

"Don't worry, Anna," Faith told her now. "You're going to win. We all know it."

"That's right," Tyler Campbell said. "We're here to see Kyle eat his words. It'll be fun."

Ray, who was supposed to stand up for Kyle in the Campbell-Malory rivalry that went back decades, chuckled. "Always is."

Kyle tried to send an apologetic look to Anna, but she didn't receive it. Anna bathed Kyle in a cool stare and turned away.

The ladies of the bunch—Bailey, Christina, Jess, Callie, and Grace—surrounded Anna and led her away. They were on her side, of course.

That left the Malory brothers facing the Campbells, like in the old days. Five against two. The Campbells, for some reason, had never thought that unfair.

Both Campbells and Malorys had grown from belligerent teens to working men, and they were all more or less friends now. But Kyle had once dated Bailey, and Ray had gone out with Christina before Christina and Grant had gotten back together. Made for some complicated friendships.

Ray ended the standoff, the Campbells grinning like hyenas, by clapping Ross on the shoulder.

"Hey, newlywed. Let me buy you boys a round of beer." He waved his hand at the Campbell brothers, and they surged toward the bar.

Adam, the lucky bastard who'd married Bailey, gave Kyle a cordial nod, but his blue eyes held a deep gleam of satisfaction. He'd snared the lovely Bailey, and Kyle hadn't.

Kyle no longer minded—let Adam be happy. As soon as Adam had returned to Riverbend, Kyle had seen the writing on *that* wall. Bailey hadn't been able to keep her eyes off Adam, and Adam had boiled with jealousy every time Kyle came near her.

He'd realized the two were madly in love, and he'd backed off. Not easily, but he'd conceded the field. Now Adam and Bailey had a happy marriage and an adorable kid.

Kyle sent Adam a returning grin. He had no more interest in Bailey.

The lovely young woman with blond hair, very blue eyes, and strength of will who'd come here tonight to prove herself was another matter. Kyle found himself trying to keep Anna in sight as she moved through the bar, but the Campbell wives cut her from his view.

"Haven't seen you around much, Ray," Tyler way saying as they bellied up to the bar. "I know why I haven't seen Kyle." He sent a sympathetic look to Kyle's cane. "Healing is a bitch. But where have *you* been keeping yourself?"

To Kyle's surprise, Ray flushed and flicked his eyes sideways. "Here and there. Lot's to do."

Kyle frowned at the evasive answer. The ranch, while always busy, hadn't been unusually so. Even before Kyle's injury, Ray had decided not to do the entire rodeo circuit this year, choosing venues close to home and riding for fun. Which meant he had a lot of free time these days.

So where had Ray been disappearing to? *A woman,* was Kyle's first guess, but Ray never hid his girlfriends, and he definitely didn't sneak around with another guy's lady. Grant and Christina had been broken up for almost a year before Ray had asked Christina out.

Kyle clocked his brother's half-embarrassed reaction plus his relief when Tyler dropped the subject. He tucked away the information and resolved to find out later what was going on.

Meanwhile …

"You really challenged Dr. Anna to ride the mechanical

bull?" Tyler asked. "Are you crazy? She'll stay on it for an hour and then make it follow her around. You know how good she is with animals."

"It's a *machine*," Kyle said while Tyler broke into laughter. "I'm trying to prove a point, is all."

Tyler's eyes twinkled. "What, that Dr. Anna is smarter than you and always will be?"

Ray laughed loudly, happy the topic was off him. "Kyle never learns."

"You two are assholes." Kyle accepted a beer from the bartender—who also was laughing—and drank deeply. "I didn't coerce her. We have a bet."

Tyler nodded. "Yeah, that when you lose, you'll do all kinds of shit jobs for her. Literally involving shit. Poor Kyle. You are so in for it, dude."

Even during the height of the Campbell-Malory feud, Kyle had gotten along best with Tyler. He was more easy-going and party-loving than the wall of Adam, Grant, and Carter.

But Kyle suddenly wished the feud would reignite so he could punch Tyler on the nose. Tyler's too good-looking face was creased with a wide smile, delight that Kyle would make himself a laughingstock.

"I'm done with you losers." Kyle backed away with his beer, looking for somewhere safer to drink.

His brother and Tyler boomed laughs as he went. So glad he could provide them good entertainment.

Kyle wove through the crowd, making for the back room. The line to ride the bull was already long. A tourist was on it now, a guy with what Kyle called "office pallor," probably from some snowy city up north.

The guy wasn't doing too bad, his friends yelling and

cheering for him. He had his head down, concentrating, which was the only way to do it. One second at a time, learning the feel, going with the animal.

The best bulls twisted like demons, doing anything to get the man-flea off their backs. Mechanical bulls would never be the same. While they could rotate and buck randomly, they didn't have the feel of two thousand pounds of angry flesh and blood under your butt.

Bulls quivered with life and energy—all that fury against you—and Kyle knew he'd always lose. The test was how long Kyle could endure against an animal who didn't give a shit about him and not only wanted him gone but would do his damnedest to make him regret ever thinking he could best a bull.

Kyle had no illusions that what he rode wasn't forty times stronger and faster than he was. Any idea that bulls were stupid was totally wrong too. They were smarter and more cunning than a lot of people Kyle knew.

The thrill of bull riding was stealing those few seconds, riding danger, showing how good he could be. At the end of every rodeo, Kyle went around to the bull pens and said hello, paying his respects. The bulls gave him sneering looks in return, knowing they were the superior species.

The guy on the mechanical bull finally finished. The bull wound down and his friends helped him off, laughing and joking. A woman—girlfriend or wife—hugged him on the way out.

The Campbell women led Anna forward, her turn next. Kyle found a place to set down his beer and hobbled toward them, wincing when people bumped his still-healing body.

"You can do this, Anna," Callie said as they surged around the waiting bull, its plastic face in no way menacing.

"Just hang on and tell it what to do," Jess said with a grin.

"Yeah, teach my brother not to mess with you," Grace added.

Kyle scowled at her. "Oh, come on. I thought at least my sweet baby sister would take my side."

"Not when your side is wrong." Grace's eyes sparkled in lively anticipation. "Make me proud, Anna."

Kyle shook his head. "Marrying Carter has made you a hard woman."

"She's not hard at all," Carter Sullivan said, more or less in Kyle's ear. "I like her just the way she is."

Kyle turned to find Carter right behind him, not crowding him exactly, but not backing off either. Carter was crazy protective of Grace, which was fine with Kyle most of the time, but he could be a little obsessive.

"I was joking," Kyle said, speaking slowly and carefully. "Me and Grace, we do that."

Carter gave him a nod that said, *Okay, but I'm watching.*

Bailey was speaking softly and rapidly to Anna, who'd gone almost as pale as the tourist guy from up north.

She looked scared. Anna Lawler never looked scared, no matter what kind of beast she had to face. She'd go toe-to-toe with some of the most hard-bitten ranch hands he'd ever met, and take no shit from the biggest animals in the county.

But as she assessed the mechanical bull her face pinched and she looked as though she was about to be sick.

"Anna." Kyle stepped forward. His stick struck the edge of the landing pads around the bull, and he stumbled. Hands grabbed him to keep him from falling—the soft hands of Callie and Jess, the harder ones of Carter.

Kyle regained his balance and broke away from them.

"Anna, you don't have to ride if you don't want to," he said quickly. "It's just a stupid bet."

Color returned to Anna's cheeks as she faced him. "No, I'm doing this. I don't go back on my word."

"Yeah, but maybe I don't want to see you get hurt."

Anna's eyes flashed, the sparkle of determination returning. "You get hurt all the time." She glanced pointedly at his walking stick. "At least there are pads for me to land on. And I'm *not* forfeiting by walking away."

The glare she sent him shouted anger, pride, stubbornness. She had tenacity—Kyle gave her that.

He firmed his mouth. "All right. Climb up there and fall off. Be my guest."

"I think that's what started this argument in the first place. Bailey, help me on."

Bailey shot Kyle a grin. He and Bailey had become friends again after Bailey had dumped Kyle like an unwanted sock to latch on to Adam, but right now Bailey was on Anna's side. They all were, he realized. They loved her.

Be nice if someone loved *him*.

Kyle stepped up on the mat successfully and reached Anna's side as Bailey poised to give Anna a boost.

"If you feel yourself go," Kyle said, "I mean seriously start to fall, go with it. Don't fling your hands out to stop yourself —that's how you break wrists and dislocate shoulders. Tuck those arms around you and roll as you hit. Spreads out the impact."

Anna's eyes rounded. "These pads are six inches thick."

"Doesn't matter. You fall wrong, you still break something. Trust me. I've fallen all kinds of wrong and broken a lot of bones."

"No kidding." Another glance at his creaking torso. "And yet, you still do it."

Kyle forced a shrug. "It's the challenge. Plus a nice amount of money I can put into the ranch."

"It's still crazy." Anna squared her shoulders. "Get me onto this thing, Bailey."

The mechanical bull was nowhere near as big as a real one, but Anna gladly accepted Bailey's leg up. She patted the molded bull's neck as she settled on its back. "Don't worry, boy. I'm not here to hurt you."

As laughter rippled through the gathered crowd, Kyle positioned himself next to Anna's knee, a nice curve in her form-hugging jeans.

"Get a firm hold, but not too tight," he advised. "The strap is for balance, not for taking your entire weight. Squeeze with your knees and lower legs, like riding a horse. Keep the other hand well out of the way—you can't touch the bull with it or you forfeit."

Bailey poked him in the arm. "Stop fussing at her. Anna knows what she's doing."

"This isn't the same." Kyle gave the plastic beast a warning glare. "Not at all the same."

"Go away, Kyle," Anna stated. "Let me make a fool of myself on my own."

Kyle wanted to reach up and pull her off into his arms, carry her away from the throng eager to see Anna put Kyle in his place. He kept imagining Anna falling, landing on her slim shoulder or hip, spending the next six weeks in a body cast, or falling completely wrong and breaking her neck. All because Kyle couldn't keep his mouth shut.

Bailey tugged at him. "Come on. We have to move."

Kyle gave Anna a last look and reluctantly followed Bailey out of the safety zone to the barroom floor.

Anna wrapped one hand around the strap and gave the manager who operated the bull a thumbs-up. Kyle held his breath as the bull started to move.

Dino's manager had a lot of experience with his mechanical bull. He knew how to start it slowly, how to keep it gentle for absolute beginners. No one had ever gotten hurt riding here, but there was always a first time.

The bull moved tentatively at first, easy bucks, mild spins. Anna hung on without much trouble, then she gave the man another thumbs-up.

"Let it rip!" she shouted.

The man grinned. "All right. Here we go!"

"What's he doing?" Kyle demanded of Bailey as the bull sped up.

"Anna told him she wanted a real ride. That's what your bet is, isn't it? That she can't stay ten seconds on a rampaging bull?"

"Yeah, but …"

"I think she'll be okay, Kyle. Anna isn't stupid."

"No, she's a frigging genius, but she's also pissed off at me."

Bailey glanced at him with the deep brown eyes Adam had fallen madly in love with. "Really? I can't imagine why."

"Stop her," Kyle growled. He glared at the manager and made a slicing motion across his throat. "Kill it."

Too late. Anna yelped as the bull bucked like the wildest ride Kyle had straddled out of a chute. The braid she'd coiled around her head came loose and flopped on her back like a golden rope.

Her head jerked, as did her arm. The fake bull spun and

twisted, bucked and rocked. Anna held on grimly, eyes wide, yells escaping her mouth.

Three seconds, Kyle counted, breath held. *Four, five ... Come on, you can do it. Five more and we can stop this.*

On second number seven, Anna slipped. Kyle involuntarily moved forward as though he could hold her on.

Anna came loose from the bull and gave a piercing shriek as she flew through the air. She landed in a loose tangle of limbs, her unbound hair spilling over her like a silken cloud.

The manager quickly stopped the bull, and it swayed to a halt, chest down, the wild animal now comically paralyzed and so obviously fake.

Kyle was next to Anna before he remembered moving. He left his walking stick who-knew-where, and his healing ribs creaked as he went down on one knee beside her.

Anna rolled over, flipping her hair out of her way. "Damn!" she said in a loud voice. "I lost."

"No, you didn't." Kyle clenched his fists to keep from touching her. "You were on there a while before it sped up. It all counts."

Anna sat up, looking none the worse for wear. "The time didn't start until it really bucked. I'm not going to wimp out of a bet, Kyle Malory, in front of the entire county. You make a reservation, and I'll go buy a decent dress."

She allowed herself to take Kyle's hand so he could help her to her feet as the bar cheered her like she was a superhero. But the flinty gaze Anna sent Kyle told him he faced a date with him with the same enthusiasm she would a root canal without pain killer.

ANNA CHECKED HER DRESS AND HAIR, MAKEUP, SHOES, AND jewelry for the twentieth time as she waited a few nights later for Kyle to pick her up.

She stood in the bedroom of the compact house she'd bought from Bailey Campbell upon returning to Riverbend from San Angelo. Anna liked the cheerful rooms set one behind the other, the small patch of garden, and the neighbor, Mrs. Kaye, always ready with leftover soup and gossip when Anna came home from a long, tough day.

"Are the earrings too much?" Anna asked the cat who lay in the exact center of her bed. He was a short-haired tuxedo kitty Anna had rescued in San Angelo, a scrawny, starving kitten full of worms and fleas. Patches had become Anna's devoted friend, which meant he was happy to blink lazily at her from the bed as she fretted.

"Too much," Anna decided.

She pulled out the dangling gold hoops, threw them to the dresser, and stuck in tiny gold studs. There. Not too ostentatious, but the hint of gold looked nice with her hair up.

Wait, should she keep her hair up? Was it too severe? Or should she brush it out in a natural fall? Anna usually wore her hair in a braid pinned up to keep it out of the way as she worked. She ought to just hack her hair off entirely for convenience, but she touched it now, knowing she was too fond of it for that.

She sighed. "Hair stays up. What about the dress? Is it too short? I could just wear nice pants and a top."

Patches yawned, lowered his head, and closed his eyes.

The dress was dark blue and hugged her curves, what there was of them. Anna's physical work and little time for meals left her lean and tough, but her breasts were lean too.

She eyed them in the high-necklined dress—no showing off what she didn't have.

It wasn't like she was trying to impress Kyle Malory with her figure, she told herself. He had big-bosomed women flinging themselves at him right, and left, and center, some so busty they barely fit into their tight "I Love You Kyle" T-shirts. He'd barely notice Anna in her slim but modest dress, but she wasn't about to wave her tits at him.

The sleeveless sheath came with a little jacket that hid her tanned arms, her skin scarred from years of working with animals. Few animals bit or scratched her deliberately, but there were always mishaps.

She observed her shrimpy body with a sigh. The dress looked a little bit sexy—but again, why did she care whether Kyle found her sexy?

Resolutely she shrugged on the jacket. Great, now she looked like she was on her way to church.

Anna was about to slide the jacket off again, when head-lights flashed through the living room window and a purring motor paused in front of the house. Anna jumped, slammed the jacket closed, and grabbed her bag-like purse.

"See you, Patches."

The cat opened one eye then closed it again, settling in for a nap, as Anna charged out onto the porch.

Chapter Five

❦

K yle parked the Lexus he'd rented for the evening in front of Anna's house and climbed stiffly from it.

Finally cleared by his doctor to drive, Kyle had called Karen Marvin—always a dangerous undertaking—for her recommendation on a luxury car for his date. With Karen's need to have the best in everything, he figured she'd know.

Karen hadn't been at Dino's but she'd heard about Anna's ride and her bet with Kyle. Karen tortured him by demanding the full story then directed him to a dealer in White Fork, who'd rented Kyle the plushest car he'd ever ridden in. The thing practically drove itself, alerting Kyle when cars approached and slowing down automatically if he got too close to the vehicle ahead of him.

When Anna stepped out onto the porch of the little shotgun house, Kyle forgot about the car, the bet, and the rest of his life.

Golden rays of the setting sun caught and haloed Anna's hair. Her blue dress shimmered as she moved, its hem showing a nice amount of leg. Her hair was pinned up as usual, baring her graceful neck, tiny gold earrings glittering. Her high-heeled pumps made her walk carefully, completing the picture of elegance.

His heart beat faster as he watched Anna descended the steps, his feet rooted to the sidewalk. A movement next door caught his eye—Mrs. Kaye had come out to her porch, pretending to look at the sunset.

"Oh, hello, Kyle," the woman said. "Good evening, Anna. Are you two going out? Have a good time."

She watched with unabashed interest as Kyle hobbled around the car to the passenger door and Anna stepped serenely off the porch.

A buckle bunny would have gushed about the car and dived right in to play with the bells and whistles. Anna only gave the Lexus a passing glance and waved at Mrs. Kaye.

"Thanks, Mrs. Kaye," she said. "You have a good night."

Kyle held the door while Anna slid inside. She reached for the handle to close it herself, yanking it out of Kyle's grip.

Stifling a sigh, Kyle gave Mrs. Kaye a polite good night and moved to the driver's side. Mrs. Kaye watched with great enjoyment. If the rest of Riverbend hadn't known Kyle was taking Anna out tonight, they would now.

He said nothing as he put the car in gear and smoothly pulled away from the curb. Anna said nothing either. Was going to be a hell of a long night if neither of them spoke.

"Take us about twenty minutes to get to Chez Orleans," Kyle said into the awkward silence as they went around the town's square. "We have a reservation for seven thirty."

"Mmm-hmm."

Kyle clutched the steering wheel and gritted his teeth. Of course she already knew that. If he could not be an idiot for the rest of the night, that'd be good.

The sun sank as Kyle drove out of Riverbend, the edge of its round, orange disk disappearing over the tallest hill. Dusk settled around them, and the car's headlights politely flicked themselves on.

Kyle considered the Hill Country at its prettiest in twilight. The sky took on a deep blue hue, and the sun stained clouds on the horizon a brilliant hot pink and higher, thinner clouds gold. The contrast of the darkening land to the amazing sky always entranced him.

The car beeped, and Anna jumped.

"Just means someone's passing us." Kyle slowed as a jacked-up pickup pulled out beside them on the two-lane road and roared past. The pickup's driver narrowly missed an oncoming truck, which had to dive onto the shoulder to avoid a collision.

"Haynes boys," Kyle said as he recognized the truck, a new one they'd been flashing around. "Assholes."

"They have a ranch west of town," Anna said. "And yes, they are assholes."

He glanced at her. "You go out there to see their cattle?"

"I see everyone's cattle," she answered. "I certainly wouldn't go to their ranch for any other reason."

"Yeah, I know that." Kyle's grip on the steering wheel tightened in irritation. "I was just making conversation."

"At least I mostly deal with their manager," Anna said, sounding grateful. "I don't have to put up with the Hayneses themselves."

"They took over the old Morgan place. Morgan family moved to San Antonio when their granddaddy died and rented out the land."

"I know," Anna said. "I grew up here."

5

Kyle shot her an annoyed glance. "Do you have to argue with *everything* I say?"

Anna lifted her hands. "Sorry. What do you usually talk to your girlfriends about?"

"Not a lot," Kyle admitted.

"I can't be surprised. I've seen some of them."

A fair hit. Many of the girls who wanted to bang a bull rider weren't gifted with a ton of brains. Those on the smart side also just wanted to bang a bull rider, and didn't much want Kyle to talk.

"I went out with Bailey for a while," Kyle pointed out. "She's nice *and* has a brain."

"Yes, I like Bailey. And then she dumped your butt for Adam."

Kyle growled in his throat. "I like to think it was a mutual decision."

"I'm giving you a hard time." Anna actually sent him a little smile. "Bailey told me the whole story."

Great. "I hope I came out of it somewhat good."

Anna nodded. "I heard how you gallantly backed away and told Adam to propose to her. So, yes, you get props."

"Aw, thanks."

"I suppose you can make a good decision every once in a while," Anna said serenely.

"Okay, seriously, are you ever going to cut me a break?"

Anna shrugged. "I don't know. Maybe if— Oh, crap. Look at that."

Kyle jerked his eyes forward, stepping hard on the brakes. He saw what Anna did, a pickup half overturned in a ditch. Behind it, on its side, was a horse trailer. The pickup's headlights were off, but one of the blinkers was stuck on, flashing golden slices through the darkness.

No other vehicle was in sight, but Kyle knew in his bones that the Haynes boys were responsible for this wreck. No one else had passed them since the Haynes truck, and it would be just like them to run someone off the road and then fly on by.

He quickly pulled over. Anna was out of the car the moment he stopped, making sure all was clear before she ran across the road in her high heels. Kyle followed, cursing his injuries for slowing him down.

He recognized the woman who shakily pulled herself out of the pickup—Sherrie Bates. She and her husband ran a small head of cattle way south of Riverbend. They were in their thirties, with kids who went to school with Faith.

"Sherrie?" Kyle reached for her. "Take it easy."

Sherrie clutched at Kyle. "My horse …" She tried to jerk from him, to move toward the overturned trailer from which a horse's shrill cries sounded, but she wavered on her feet, her breath ragged.

"Hush now." Kyle put one comforting arm around her. "I'll call Ross—he's working tonight. And you lucked out—that's Dr. Anna." He pointed to Anna who was already picking her way to the trailer. "She'll make sure your horse is okay."

"Came right at me." Sherrie rested one trembling hand on the canted pickup. "Don't know who it was. Headlights—all I could see."

"I know. They were driving like crazy. I'm getting Ross." He showed Sherrie his phone as he tapped Ross's name on his contacts.

He heard Anna struggling with the latch on the horse trailer. The horse was alive at least, but wailing and kicking.

If it thrashed around too much it could break limbs or cut itself up.

Anna was talking to it, doing her horse-whisperer thing, but the latch rattled and wouldn't open. Sherrie started for the trailer again, but Kyle held her back. If the horse was badly hurt, or dying, she didn't need to see that.

"Ross?" Kyle said into the phone as Ross Campbell answered. "Accident on the 2626, about halfway between Riverbend and Llano. No, I'm fine—I was just passing. It's Sherrie Bates and one of her horses. Anna's here but we'll need a horse trailer and an EMT to look after Sherrie. Seems likes she's okay, but..."

As Kyle spoke calmly to keep Sherrie reassured, Ross on the other end was yelling orders. He'd become interim sheriff after the last one got himself busted, and was running for sheriff in the election in November, not that far off. The sheriff's department under Ross's hand, as young as he was, now ran like oiled clockwork.

Ross finished and returned to Kyle. "Lots of stuff heading your way. I also alerted the Llano County sheriff's office. Did you see what happened?"

"Pretty sure it was the Haynes boys being reckless as usual. Might want to speak to them."

"Thanks, Kyle." Ross didn't promise one way or another, but Kyle heard the grim note in his voice.

Kyle had no way to prove the Hayneses had run Sherrie off the road, though the odds were they'd done it. But unless Sherrie had seen them clearly or had a dash cam that could show exactly what happened they'd get away with it.

"Kyle?" Anna's voice floated to him. "Can you give me a hand?"

Sherrie started, panic in her eyes, but Kyle gently steadied her. "Stay put. We'll hear sirens any second. Anna and I got this."

Sherrie nodded. When Kyle finally released her, she rested against the cool side of the truck as though drawing comfort from its solid weight.

Kyle clicked on the flashlight on his cell phone and made his way around the back of the truck to the trailer. It lay on its side in a ditch about three feet deep, a trickle of water and slick mud making footing tricky.

Anna struggled with the latch that held the trailer closed. By the light of Kyle's phone, he saw that the accident had bent the door, wedging the bolt in place. The horse, kicking on the other side, wasn't helping.

Anna crooned to it at the same time she tugged at the latch. "It's all right, Camden. I'll get you out."

She knew the horse by name. That was Anna all over.

"How do you know which one is in there?" Kyle asked. He couldn't see much in the trailer but a horse butt and the occasional flash of wild eye. The horse was trapped on one side of the two-horse trailer, in the stall that was now on the bottom of the turned-over rig.

"Streak of white in his tail. Their other horse has a black tail."

"Good memory."

"I remember horses, is all." She pulled at the latch again. "All animals, really."

Better than she did people, Kyle figured she meant. "If you get your hands out of the way, I can get that."

She sent him an impatient look. "You're still recovering from an injury."

"I wasn't injured in my arms." Kyle reached for the latch. Anna wouldn't move, so Kyle slid his fingers beneath hers.

Her warm touch trickled fire inside him. Kyle tried to shut out the sensation and pulled at the cold metal, grunting at a dart of pain. His arms might not have been broken, but the muscles in his torso—his core, the physical therapist called it—were still weak and sore.

Anna managed not to say she'd been right, only positioned her hands above and below his. Together they pulled, jerked, yanked, rattled.

Finally the bent piece of bar worked through the catch, and the latch burst open. Anna stumbled back, right into Kyle. She fit nicely in his arms, and her hair smelled of flowers.

She squirmed instantly away from him, like she couldn't get free fast enough. The horse, secured by a halter rope, kicked and scrambled, half on his side, unable to get his legs under him. Fear radiated from him in a solid stench.

Kicking off her shoes, Anna climbed into the empty stall, which was now above the horse, her light frame barely moving the trailer. Kyle held on to the tailgate, afraid to join her in case his weight slid them farther into the ditch.

Anna reached over the partition and patted Camden, talking to him, hands working to unhook the halter rope. "Kyle," she said softly. "Can you go back to the car and get my purse? I'll need something to calm him down or we might not get him out of here without him hurting himself."

"Your purse?" Kyle blinked. "What's in there?"

"Tranquilizer. And a shot of antibiotics. Might need that too."

Kyle stared at her. "You carry horse tranquilizers around in your *purse?*"

"It's an emergency medical bag," Anna said impatiently. "I never know when I'm going to be called out."

Kyle shook himself, rearranging his thoughts. "You going to be okay here?"

"Yes—I'll keep him steady. Hurry."

Kyle released his hold of the trailer and made his painstaking way back to the pickup. He told Sherrie quickly that Camden was okay and Anna was taking care of him. Sherrie nodded gratefully, and Kyle hobbled across the dark and empty road to the Lexus, his dress pants and shoes now a muddy mess.

He lifted Anna's purse, marveling at how heavy it was. Felt like she had a hammer in there—he guessed she was prepared for a guy getting too handy.

By the time Kyle started back across the road, emergency lights flashed in the distance and sirens wailed. Moments later a sheriff's department SUV and an ambulance pulled in from the Riverbend side, a Llano County emergency vehicle from the other direction.

Ross Campbell leapt out of the River County SUV, followed by Deputy Harrison. Joe Harrison had moved to this tiny county from San Antonio in the past year, infusing a calm practicality into the sheriff's department.

Ross assessed the situation with his usual quickness. Harrison followed Kyle to the horse trailer, and Kyle craned into it to hand Anna her purse.

Anna had discarded the little jacket that went with her kickass blue dress, baring her arms to the warm night. The skirt hiked its way up her legs as she leaned over the partition to comfort the horse.

Harrison relaxed visibly when he saw Anna. "Glad you're here, Dr. Anna. You got this?"

Anna, one hand still on the horse, scrabbled inside her purse. "I think so. Tell Sherrie everything's under control."

Harrison backed away. "Good. Sure thing." He caught Kyle staring at him, and gave him a sheepish smile. "I can deal with people. Horses are another thing." He gave Kyle a nod and quickly faded toward Sherrie's truck.

Anna withdrew a small plastic case from the purse. "Kyle, can you help?"

Kyle stepped up to her. "What do you need?"

Anna handed him the case. "Take out the syringe, then break the seal on that vial. Carefully."

Kyle felt like his hands were three times their size as he dug out the plastic syringe and handed it to her as though it were fragile porcelain. Anna flicked the protective cap from the needle with her thumb and waited while Kyle unsealed the tiny vial of clear liquid she'd indicated.

His thumbs fumbled with the seal but finally he tore it off, plastic fluttering to the grass. Anna said nothing, only jabbed the needle through the rubber on top of the bottle.

"Draw that into the syringe." She kept her hand on the horse, who continued to writhe in panic. "Don't worry about doing it perfectly, just get it in there."

Kyle had dosed animals before, not to mention taken plenty of shots himself. He hated them, though. He grimaced as he held the vial steady and drew the serum into the syringe.

He handed the syringe back to Anna. She grabbed it and jabbed the needle straight into the horse, depressing the plunger.

Kyle doubted Camden would feel the prick of the needle in his larger panic. The horse continued to kick and thrash, and then slowly, slowly, he quieted, his breathing loud in the sudden silence.

"I need to check him for injury and then take him out of here," Anna said. "Can you get the tailgate all the way open?"

Kyle yanked at it until he could finally move aside the bent part of the gate. His sides ached, his healing muscles not happy with him.

Anna climbed from the trailer then squashed her way into the horse's stall, worming herself forward to release Camden from the halter rope.

Kyle went cold, expecting Camden to slam into her any second. Anna could be crushed under the horse's body before Kyle could pull her to safety.

Camden's eyes were wide, but he calmed as Anna unhooked the rope from his halter. She slid her hands all over the horse, competently pressing, testing, moving, just as she'd done with Kyle when he'd landed hard in the arena.

"Nothing obviously broken," Anna announced in relief. "I'm going to back him toward you. Make sure he has something solid to step on."

The tailgate now dangled from one mangled hinge. A few stomps with Kyle's boot wrenched it free, and he braced the metal ramp on the hard earth of the ditch.

Anna showed the horse where to put his feet, first inside the trailer, then on the ramp. The tricky part was to get him to swivel his hindquarters so he'd emerge standing up.

Camden was sedated enough by now, though, that Anna simply placed his hooves where she wanted them to go. Kyle, on his other side, guided him out with hands on his shoulder as Anna held his head.

Slowly, slowly, one step at a time, Anna steered Camden back, talking to him the entire way. After what seemed forever, Camden stood on the flat ramp, upright, all four feet planted. He trembled but stood quietly, never flinching when Anna snapped the rope she'd untied back onto his halter.

"I need to get him back to my place," Anna said. "X-ray him and make damn sure nothing is fractured." She glanced at Kyle as though remembering why he was there. "Sorry, Kyle."

Kyle fought disappointment, but he agreed that the health of the horse was more important than their date—if it even was a real date.

"It's okay," he conceded. "We've missed the reservation by now anyway."

He couldn't see Anna well in the dark but felt her gaze on him, her blue eyes glistening in the waning light from his cell phone.

"Come with me?" she asked.

Chapter Six

A nna wasn't sure what made her almost beg Kyle to ride back with her. Logically, they could reschedule the date and go their separate ways, but for some reason, she didn't yet want the night to end.

Ross and Deputy Harrison took statements from Sherrie, Sherrie calming a little under Ross's care. Harrison waved in the truck and horse trailer they'd called to retrieve Camden.

Kyle told Ross he was very sure the Haynes brothers had caused the accident, but Anna couldn't commit herself. She couldn't truthfully say that she'd seen them, only that they'd nearly run another person off the road before that. Ross nodded and wrote down their observations.

Anna and Kyle loaded Camden into the trailer. Anna's new dress was ruined, she saw as she climbed out from securing the horse, the silky blue fabric stained with horse drool and grease, the skirt ripped where it had caught on a bolt. Her hands were grimy, her hair falling from its pins, and she'd probably smeared dirt on her face.

Paramedics were taking care of Sherrie, though Anna

hugged her before giving her over to the EMTs. Anna had called Sherrie's husband for her, and the panicked man was making his way to the clinic where he'd meet her.

Anna saw that the man who'd arrived with the horse trailer was Carter Sullivan. Always quiet, Carter said nothing as they loaded the horse, and he gave Anna a ready nod when she asked him to drive the horse to her office.

"See you there," Carter said calmly. He climbed back into the truck and pulled out carefully, barely bouncing the trailer.

Anna knew she could have ridden with Carter to her office, but for some reason, she headed without hesitation for Kyle's rental car, letting him open the door for her.

"You all right?" he asked as she slid inside.

"Sure," Anna tried to sound like she did this every night. An emergency with an animal was nothing new, though it had never happened to her on a date. "A mess, but okay."

Kyle flashed her a grin. "You look great. But I don't think Chez Orleans would let us in like this, even if they had a spare table in their back hall." He tugged at his suit coat, which was spattered with mud and possibly horse shit.

"Oh well. Maybe next time."

"Tell you what. We'll check Camden over and then I'll take you to the diner." Kyle shrugged at Anna's surprised look. "You need to eat."

Anna's heart beat faster, but she kept her tone nonchalant. "Will that get me off the hook for the bet?"

"Mmm, I'll think about it. Let's take one thing at a time."

Kyle shut her door and moved around the car to the driver's side, leaving Anna to catch her breath. Her head buzzed with worry and tiredness, as well as disappointment.

But that was the way of things living in ranch country,

and she'd pledged her life to taking care of its animals. They didn't get injured or sick to anyone's schedule.

She hoped Ross found the Hayneses, or whoever the other driver turned out to be, and kicked their ass.

Kyle kept Carter's taillights in view all the way to Anna's vet office. It lay just outside of town, a few miles from the Malory ranch, with a wide parking lot where clients could load and unload horses or cattle.

A small stable with a row of stalls, in which animals stayed for observation or recovery, lined one side of the lot. Anna's office, where she did her paperwork or met with owners, was in a low-ceilinged room adjacent to the stalls, but her exams and surgery happened in the building behind the stables.

That building held her operating room and the prep room next to it, and a larger box stall where mares were inseminated and delivered foals if there might be a problem. Anna did her gelding out here as well. It was a good setup, put together by the previous vet. Anna had been grateful that she'd been able to start right in.

Anna had an assistant, Janette, a young woman who loved animals and hoped to go to vet school. Janette sometimes spent the night if they had to keep an eye on certain animals, and she answered phones, held horses, and helped Anna prep and clean up from surgeries. But Janette had gone home hours ago, the office silent and empty.

Carter parked and came around to help unload Camden. Kyle had said nothing at all after he'd offered to take her to the diner, and now he assisted Carter in lowering the tailgate so Anna could back out the horse.

She didn't have the heart to call Janette in to work on a Friday night, and it turned out, she didn't have to. Kyle began to help without a word, wincing from injuries only a little as he helped position Camden against the X-ray machine.

Kyle held Camden steady, the horse calming now that he was indoors and not moving. The tranq Anna had given him had such a good effect that Camden laid his head on Kyle's shoulder and closed his eyes.

Lucky horse.

Anna finished quickly. The X-ray showed up on the computer within seconds, and she scanned through it.

"No fractures," she announced with relief.

She left the computer and ran her hands over the horse again, looking for swelling and heat but she found nothing. Camden truly had been lucky.

"I think we can take him home," she finished. "As long as he's supervised overnight." Sherrie wouldn't be in any shape to do that, nor would her husband, but they had a head rancher who helped take care of all their horses.

Carter slid out of his truck, where he'd been patiently waiting, to open the trailer to load Camden. Both Kyle and Carter were being so nice tonight, but Anna realized they weren't doing anything special for her. This was how they treated everybody.

Once they had Camden settled in the trailer, Carter rolled off with him, taking a right from Anna's driveway to head out to Sherrie's ranch.

"I should go with him," Anna said as the taillights disappeared into the darkness.

"No, you should let Carter take care of it. He has a lot of experience, he knows the guys who work on Sherrie's ranch, and he's not on a date."

Anna debated. The horse was her responsibility until she returned him to his owner, but there truly wasn't much more she could do. Carter was an expert with horses and could explain the situation.

"All right then." Anna glanced at her ruined dress in resignation. "I'll go home. I'm a mess."

"Nope. I told you—taking you to the diner. You're wiped."

"I am wiped," Anna admitted. Her knees felt weak, and she knew she'd collapse soon from release from worry. "But I'm not fit to be seen, not even in the diner."

"You go there for lunch after you've been out on ranches all morning. I see you. You don't run home and scrub yourself down and change your clothes then, do you?"

Anna had to smile. "No, but I'm not wearing a wreck of a new dress. And I at least wash my hands."

"You've done that three times since we've been here. This is Riverbend—we're more worried about our horses than what we look like. I'm taking over as your physician, and I'm prescribing one of Mrs. Ward's burgers with all the works."

"I'm vegetarian," Anna reminded him.

"Okay, then, a veggie burger with the works. She has them on the menu." Kyle's face when he said "veggie burger" made Anna want to laugh.

He was right about one thing—Anna was starving. She'd looked forward to fine cuisine at Chez Orleans, figuring a well-trained chef could fix a kickass vegetarian meal. But comfort food at Mrs. Ward's would have to do.

"Fine," she said, letting out a heartfelt sigh. "Let me lock up."

HEADS TURNED WHEN KYLE USHERED ANNA INTO THE DINER. They must be an entertaining sight—Kyle in an actual suit whose pants were mud-coated, Anna in a torn and stained dress, bits of hay in her hair. Kyle had tried to scrape his shoes free of mud and whatever crap had been in the ditch with limited success. Anna had found a pair of sneakers at her office which she wore in place of the high heels she'd begun the night in.

Those in the parking lot had stared hard at the Lexus when Kyle had pulled up. Opening the door for Anna to step from the car, sexy legs first, had been a kick. Riverbenders would get a lot of mileage out of that.

Anna knew it, from the flush on her face. Kyle led her down the main aisle to the booth at the end, far enough from other diners so their stench of horse and ditchwater wouldn't ruin their meals.

They slid into the booth and faced each other across its table. Anna had gone quiet, no more ribbing Kyle about … everything. The waitress, one of Mrs. Ward's daughters, popped out of the kitchen in record time, setting down ice water and pulling out her pad to take their order.

Anna calmly ordered the veggie burger and iced tea. Kyle asked for the biggest cheeseburger on the menu with all the fixings, and an iced tea as well.

"You don't mind if I eat meat in front of you?" Kyle asked Anna as the waitress walked away, a spring in her step.

Anna frowned as though trying to understand the question. "It's my choice. What you eat is your choice."

"So what *do* vegetarians eat?" Kyle asked in true interest. "Besides salad."

"All kinds of things," Anna answered readily. "Grains, vegetables, beans, seeds. I don't follow any special rules, I just don't base my meals around meat or dairy. A baked potato with bean chili is fine."

"That actually sounds good."

"It is good, if you make it right." Anna took a sip of her water. "But I have to read labels closely. You'd be amazed at what meat and dairy gets into."

"I thought you'd be eating, you know, tofu and stuff."

Anna wrinkled her nose. "I hate tofu. Tastes like rubber, no matter what you do to it. And the fake meat is mostly disgusting." She shuddered. "Veggie burgers are different. They're beans and chickpeas, which fry up nicely. Like falafel. Love that."

"Hard to find falafel in Riverbend."

"That's why I like to go to Austin whenever I can. They have great vegetarian restaurants."

"And steak houses."

"Yep," Anna said without rancor. "Something for everyone."

Kyle turned his water glass on the table. "You know, if we all become vegetarian, cattle ranchers will be out of business."

"Like I said, I'm not trying to convert the world," Anna said, sounding sincere. "It's *my* choice. If you saw what went on after you sold your cattle to the market, you wouldn't eat them either. But I won't talk about it—don't want to put you off your dinner."

"Thanks," Kyle said with a grimace.

Anna laughed. She was beautiful when she did that, her face lighting up, her laughter like silver.

The waitress delivered their meals after a time, and they both dug in.

Kyle liked watching Anna eat. She didn't pick at the food and pretend she wasn't hungry—she grabbed her burger with both hands and went for it. Sure, it was a veggie burger, but Anna bit into it like it was ambrosia.

"Mmm." She closed her eyes and licked her lips. "Mmm. Mmm. They know how to make them here."

Kyle grinned. "Did you teach them?"

Anna opened her eyes. "I did, as a matter of fact. It's hard to be a vegetarian in Riverbend. Mrs. Ward is always up for something new, though. Your sister—she's a great vegetarian cook. She gets it—a vegetarian meal is more than a green salad with rice."

"Grace is awesome."

Anna waited, then raised her brows when Kyle only took another bite of his very juicy, hot, well-seared burger.

"A brother proud of a sister?" she asked. "Admitting it?"

"Why not? Grace and I had our differences when she started seeing Carter, but we've moved on. Carter makes her happy. And he knows I'll break his teeth if he doesn't."

"Your family is so close."

Kyle caught the wistfulness in Anna's voice. When they'd been kids in school, Anna had been quiet, sitting in the corner reading books instead of running around screaming like the rest of them. Kyle hadn't paid much attention to her, which he regretted now.

Anna had blossomed into something beautiful, but her beauty had always been there, he realized. Just bottled away, waiting for someone to uncork it. Kyle remembered how surprised they'd all been when Callie Jones, the popular, poised debutante who won pretty much every "Most Whatever" award, had become best friends with Anna Lawler.

Callie, it turned out, had been the only one to see Anna's worth. Kyle wondered where his eyes had been, but teenagers could be stupid and self-absorbed. At least, Kyle had been. He'd focused on horses, bull riding, and learning what to do with girls who weren't his sisters. Anyone outside his radar hadn't registered.

Anna was registering now.

He wasn't sure how to respond to her observation that Kyle and his family were close. He shrugged. "I'm glad we get along. Lucy has gone a little nuts trying to be a big-city executive, but seems like she's good at it. She's making money, and she's happy. I think. Kind of hard to pin her down about that last part."

"She wants to do something on her own," Anna said. "I have to respect that. I had to strike out on my own too. I love Riverbend, but job opportunities are few and far between."

"Especially for women. If you're not a rancher ..." Kyle took another bite of his excellent burger. "Or a cook. I bet Callie could have found you a job, though."

"Maybe. We talked about it. But I really wanted to be a vet, and I had to dedicate all my time to school to do that. Plus I needed to prove myself, mostly to me. I didn't want to sit at home waiting for life to happen."

Anna's parents had moved to Houston after she'd gone off to A&M, in search of better job opportunities. It was true that if you didn't have money or a job the town depended on, you could slide into hard times. Many ranchers between here and Austin had sold up to developers and gone to live with kids or grandkids in the endless suburbs.

Anna had been an only child, which might explain some of Anna's quietness and shyness. Kyle's house had always been full of family and love, even when it had been absolute chaos and everyone shouting at each other. But behind it, they'd all known they had each other's backs.

"I remember how smart you were in school," Kyle said admiringly. "Everyone knew you'd have no trouble getting into any college you wanted. And you didn't. I had to practically beg to be let into UT and then work my ass off to stay there. I was never top of the class. But I made it. I'm proud of my bachelor's degree—framed that and hung it up high in the office."

"You didn't major in partying?" Anna asked, looking innocent. "That's what I heard."

"Okay, so there was a little of that."

"A lot, from what Grace told me."

Kyle shrugged. "Grace wasn't there. What does she know?"

"She visited you," Anna said. "She said you could barely stand up and walk to class."

"*One* time." Kyle held up a finger. "She sprang on me the morning after a long weekend. My sisters, I swear ..."

Anna laughed, again with the musical sound.

"Hey, Anna. Kyle. Sounds like you're having fun."

Kyle looked up as Christina Campbell stopped next to them, her daughter propped in the crook of her arm. The little girl's name was Emma, and she had Christina's big brown eyes and Grant's stubborn look.

"Hey, Christina," Anna said brightly.

Did Anna sound super glad to see Christina? As in *So happy you're here to rescue me from this asshole?*

Anna reached up and poked Emma in the tummy. Emma's smile blossomed. "Hi!" she shouted.

"Hi back," Anna said. "You're friendly."

Christina bounced her daughter, her fond look heart-melting. "She's learning how to say hello to everyone."

Emma stared hard at Kyle then waved a chubby hand. "Hi!"

How did that arrogant some-bitch Grant Campbell have

such a cute daughter? Oh, yeah, easy. Christina was her mom.

Kyle waggled his fingers at the girl. "Hi, Emma. How you doing?"

Christina looked back and forth between Anna and Kyle, noting their messed-up semi-formal attire and Anna's harried look. "*Oh,* I'm sorry. I'm interrupting. Is this the famous date?"

"Uh, no," Kyle said.

At the same moment, Anna said, "Yes, it is."

Chapter Seven

✿

"No," Kyle repeated in a louder voice, his determination rising. "This is us eating 'cause we're hungry."

"It counts," Anna said defiantly. "There was an accident on the highway and we missed our reservation at Chez Orleans. But the diner is good enough for me."

"I see." Christina gave them another long look while Emma continued to wave at Anna then Kyle. "I heard about the accident. Grant says Ross is sure the Haynes boys are responsible. Ross is pretty pissed off."

"Me too," Anna said. "We had to take care of Sherrie's horse, which is why we're here instead of a fancy French restaurant. But it counts." She shot a glance at Kyle.

No, it didn't count. Kyle wanted his date—a real one. But they'd have to argue about it later.

"Well, I'll leave you to it," Christina said, her expression knowing. "Oh, there's Ray." She lowered her voice to a whisper. "Kyle, who *is* that?"

Kyle followed Christina's gaze to the front of the restaurant, where his brother had just walked in, taking off his hat as the door closed behind him. His clothes were marked with white dust as though he'd been working with wallboard, and paint stained his boots.

That was weird enough, but then Ray politely turned to usher in a young woman Kyle had never seen before. She had dark hair pulled into a sloppy ponytail, a friendly face, and blue eyes that quickly took in the diner with some trepidation. She wasn't from Riverbend, that was certain.

Behind her came a lanky, leggy girl maybe a little older than Faith. The girl closely resembled the woman, no debate that she was her daughter.

"I have no idea who she is," Kyle said in irritation. "I haven't seen Ray around much lately, which is getting aggravating."

Anna turned in her seat. "Oh, that's Drew." She waved. The young woman noticed Anna, recognized her with some relief, and waved back.

Anna turned around again, blinking in surprise as she encountered Christina's and Kyle's puzzled stares.

"Drew Paresky," she continued, as though explaining what everyone should know. "She took over the bed and breakfast out on the western road."

"The derelict one from a hundred years ago?" Kyle asked. "Owned by that crazy old guy?"

"Fifty years ago. That crazy old guy was Drew's grandfather," Anna said. "She inherited the house when he passed away this summer."

Christina studied Drew with interest. "She didn't grow up here."

Anna shook her head. "Her grandparents divorced, and

her dad was raised by her grandmother in Chicago. Her father rarely came back to Riverbend, and Drew has never been here."

"How do you know all this?" Kyle asked in amazement. He hadn't heard a word about Drew Paresky, but then, he'd been penned up trying to heal for the last month. Ray hadn't said a damned thing.

"They called me to examine a cat they'd found. Poor thing was hungry and needed worming and a flea bath, but she's fine now." Anna shrugged. "You get to know people when you treat their animals."

"Looks like Ray is getting to know her too," Christina said with interest.

"Hi!" Emma yelled across the room, wildly waving her tiny hand.

Ray glanced their way, then stiffened. He nodded in acknowledgement but turned his back to sit down with Drew and her daughter in a booth on the far end of the diner.

"Huh," Christina said. "I guess he didn't want to interrupt your date. But I feel a need to be nosy coming over me. See you guys."

"Bye!" Emma called over her mother's shoulder, her fingers clenching and unclenching as Christina strode off across the diner toward Ray and company.

Anna turned back to Kyle. "You really didn't know anything about Drew?"

"Nope." Kyle picked up the last of his now-cool burger. "Ray's been keeping this a deep, dark secret."

Across the room, Ray looked uncomfortable as Christina stopped by their table and Emma did her hollered greeting.

Drew's daughter grinned at Emma in delight, and Drew brightened, but Ray sat there like a glowering lump.

"I am so giving him hell for this." Kyle's spirits lifted and he chuckled. "Now, for our argument. This isn't our date, Anna. You're not getting out of it that easy."

Anna's face lost color. "I am eating in public with you, by ourselves. That's a date."

"Not if we pay for our own meals. Then it's just two friends having a bite at the diner."

"You rented a car, put on a suit, and are driving me around," Anna pointed out.

"Started that way." Kyle downed the last of his burger and took a big slurp of iced tea. "But didn't end up that way. We were interrupted, so we have to try again. Unless the idea of talking to me over a table one more time is that bad for you."

Kyle spoke lightly, but his heart beat faster. Would she laugh at him and say no way in hell?

This was a date, and Kyle knew it. It counted. But if Kyle conceded, then he might never get to go out with her again. Obligating her to fulfill the bet meant he wouldn't have to summon the courage to ask her out and then cringe when she turned him down.

"I'll think about it," Anna said. "Though I don't mind paying for my own burger tonight. This is *good*."

"I was kidding about that," Kyle said quickly. "I got this."

Anna's eyes glinted as she licked her fingers. "Then this is our date."

"Damn it." Kyle glowered. "If I let you pay, no one in this diner will let me live it down."

"Just explain we're *not* on a date. We're sharing a meal, as friends."

"It's an old-fashioned town. They expect the guy to pick up the check, no matter what."

"No they won't. Friends eat together even in old-fashioned towns."

Kyle sat back. "I'm not going to win this one, am I?"

"Nope."

There was something else in Anna's eyes, a slight worry he couldn't place. Maybe because another old-fashioned idea said that if a woman had her meal paid for she had to put out?

Plenty of guys he knew still thought that way. Kyle never had, but then he'd not had to worry about coercing women to be with him. Girls had jumped *his* bones, whether he bought them meals or not.

But Anna had been so shy. He didn't know what her life had been like when she'd left Riverbend—had she run into guys who'd tried to enforce the put-out rule after they'd bought her dinner?

Kyle's anger boiled up. He was suddenly furious at the men she'd gone out with, whoever they were.

"You know what?" he said. "You're right. This is just two friends meeting up at the diner to eat some good burgers. We split the check, and the town can suck it."

Anna's smile returned, the look in her eyes changing to gratitude. "Deal."

"But you still owe me a date."

"Maybe." Anna sat back, dabbing her mouth with her napkin. "Like I said, I'll think about it."

She might take a couple years to do the thinking. Well, Kyle would simply have to remind her about it whenever he could.

Or, call her out to the ranch every time one of their

animals so much as shed a hair. He'd keep her number at the top of his contacts, just in case.

———————

THEY SPLIT THE CHECK, EARNING A FLICK OF EYEBROWS FROM the waitress and a keen look from Mrs. Ward at the cash register. Even their mud-stained semi-formal clothes didn't generate as much shock as Anna paying for her own meal, Anna realized. Kyle had been right about that.

Kyle walked Anna to the car and gallantly opened the passenger door for her. He moved to the driver's side and slid in, nodding through the window at more townsfolk who'd stopped to ogle them.

There was Hal Jenkins, who'd helped Anna suit up as a rodeo clown and get into the ring the day Kyle had fallen. With him was Jack Hillman, a biker and one of the town's bad boys. Jack openly stared at Kyle and then Anna beside him in astonishment.

Kyle started the car, which hummed, and pulled sedately out.

Once they hit the street, Kyle and Anna burst out laughing.

"Told you," Kyle said. "Shit, did you see their faces?"

"Biggest shock they've had since Texas stopped being a republic."

"I was going to say since Riverbend got an enforced speed limit," Kyle returned. "But yours is better. What was the biggest surprise, you think? That I didn't pick up the tab or that I didn't drink any beer?"

"I think it was you in a suit," Anna said. "Or me in a dress."

"Honey, seeing you in that dress only floored them in a good way."

Anna warmed. She wasn't supposed to like it when a guy told her she looked fine, but from growly Kyle, who could have any woman he snapped his fingers for, the compliment sank deep.

"Aw," she said lightly. "That's almost sweet."

"More than sweet." Kyle turned a corner and then pulled the car to a curb. "Well, this is you."

The disadvantage to a meal at the diner was that Anna's house lay only a block away. She could have walked home, but she hadn't had the heart to stroll away from Kyle, leaving him alone in the big fancy car.

Also, if she'd walked, every other woman in the diner might have rushed to Kyle and begged him to drive her home. Maybe there was some of that in Anna's decision too.

Mrs. Kaye's house next door was dark—she liked to be in bed by ten.

Anna hopped out as soon as Kyle stopped, but he turned off the engine, slid out, and escorted her to the porch. Anna, in her pre-date nervousness, had forgotten to turn on the porch light before she left, and now they stood in shadows.

A lump formed in Anna's throat. "Night didn't turn out like we thought."

Kyle gave her a slow nod. "True. Though it was a hell of a lot more exciting than most of my dates."

Anna wasn't sure how to take that. "I thought we agreed it wasn't a date."

"We did. It's not."

They paused, staring at each other.

Would he try to kiss her? If so, then she could claim this as their date and be off the hook.

Why did that disappoint her so much? When Kyle had said they'd have a date do-over, Anna had pretended to argue but hadn't blatantly turned him down. The idea of going out with him again, in truth and not just to fulfill a bet, did weird things to her heart.

Or did Kyle expect more tonight? They were at her house, and Anna lived alone. It was dark, and no one would notice him glide inside with her.

He might peel off what was left of her dress with his work-roughened hands, skim his touch down her arms, her breasts, her thighs.

Anna started to shake. She imagined sliding her hands under his coat, unbuttoning his shirt to find the warmth of his chest and the thump of his heart.

That wasn't the only thing she wanted to feel. She pictured unbuckling and unzipping his pants, delving in to discover how big he really was. The idea of him in her hands made her blood hot, her knees weak.

Kyle cleared his throat, and Anna jumped, breathless from the vivid fantasy.

"Okay then," he said. "Good night."

Kyle started to turn away. To go.

Anna grabbed the lapels of his coat, dragged him against her, and kissed him hard on the mouth.

It wasn't the best kiss ever. Anna missed part of his lips and landed on his cheek, the rough of his whiskers against her tongue.

Kyle laughed softly, his breath hot. He steadied her with hard hands on her arms and repositioned the kiss.

His mouth was slow, leisurely. He brushed her lips, darting inside with his tongue, soft and sweet, not intrusive.

Kyle was an excellent kisser. He knew how to tease her

mouth open but not too aggressively, how to feather kisses across her lips, how to pull her close but not crush her against him.

Anna gripped Kyle's arms, finding hard muscle under his suit, a living man hot and strong. His kiss opened something inside her, a place of longing she'd never touched, never investigated.

Kyle Malory, the man she'd thought embodied the worst in the male of the species, stood on her dark porch and soothed her heart, warmed her body, and kissed her like she was the most special woman in Riverbend.

He was taller than Anna but he leaned to her expertly, not letting her feel they were mismatched. Anna fit well against him, the largeness of him never overwhelming her.

She let herself live the imagined pleasure of sliding her hands inside his coat, fingers landing on the thin shirt over his ribs.

Kyle sucked in a breath and broke the kiss, his grip tightening on her arms.

"Damn," he said. "Keep forgetting I got hurt."

"Sorry." Anna quickly let go of him, though she did not step back. "You're still healing."

"Yeah, it's a bitch." Kyle brushed another hot-as-hell kiss over her lips then let out a sigh. "Oh, well. Good night, Anna."

He released her but didn't move. He gazed at her as time stretched, then he smoothed back a lock of her hair. His touch was warm, gentle, but his fingers shook a little, as though he held himself back.

Whenever he didn't hold back, what would it be like? Anna went fiery hot, imagining even the slightest bit.

Kyle brushed his knuckle over her cheek and then turned

with a show of reluctance and made his slow way down the porch's two steps.

"Good night," Anna called softly after him.

Kyle lifted his hand, gave her a nod and a smile and made for the car.

He waited until Anna had dug her keys out of her cavernous purse and walked safely into the house before he drove away, headlights slicing across her neighbors' yards. Anna watched him from the living room window, dropping the curtain only after his taillights disappeared around the corner.

All her strength deserted her, and she flopped to the sofa, not bothering with the lights. A weight landed on her chest, which settled itself and purred.

"Hey there," Anna scratched Patches behind the ears. She touched her lips, which still tingled from Kyle's intense and amazing kisses, and shivered. "Wow. I don't think I'll be sleeping much tonight."

———

ANNA WOKE IN THE MORNING IN HER BED, BUT SHE'D BEEN right about the nearly sleepless night.

She'd dragged herself into the bedroom, stripped off the dress, and crawled under the sheets, but every single second of darkness was filled with thoughts of Kyle. She relived again and again the moments he'd loomed over her on the dark porch, his laughter warming as he kissed her.

He'd changed her awkward kiss into something amazing, fun, enchanting. Kyle's lazy smile had turned her inside out.

Every touch, every nuance, replayed itself for the rest of the night, making Anna groggy when her phone rang at six in the morning. She crawled out of hazy dreams of Kyle and his touch and reached for the phone.

"Anna speaking," she said, trying to be polite. She was a vet, the only one around, on-call all the time.

"Hey, Dr. Anna, this is Jarrod Haynes. I think we need to talk."

Chapter Eight

❧

Anna came wide awake and sat up, dislodging Patches who glared at her and stomped to the bottom of the bed.

"What's up?" Anna managed to say to Jarrod.

She remembered the pickup charging around them on the dark road, Kyle growling that it was the Haynes boys and they were assholes. Then Sherrie's truck, the overturned horse trailer, the terrified screams of the horse trapped within.

Had Jarrod recognized Anna and Kyle in the car and realized they would have figured it out? Was he calling to threaten her, to find out what she'd seen?

Anna's worry evaporated in a rush of anger. If one of the Hayneses had caused the accident, they needed to take responsibility. She wasn't going to shy away from that.

"Yes?" she prompted when Jarrod didn't answer right away.

"We got some steers with the scours. Can you come check them out? Give them a jab so we can turn them out again?"

The scours was another way of saying the cattle had diarrhea. That could be caused by too-wet pastures or dirty
feeding areas and overcrowding—cattle infected each other
with bacteria. Could be a minor thing easily treated or an
entire herd depressed, stressed, and ill.

"What?" Anna shook herself into professional mode. "Oh.
Yeah, sure."

"Did I wake you up?" Jarrod sounded almost contrite.
Almost. "Sorry. I know it's early, but Virgil wants them back
on the range, so he threw it to me to call you. My brother's a
butthead."

Anna had been woken far earlier to help horses foal, save
dogs and cats, or treat an ailing dairy cow at milking time.
Six a.m. was nothing.

"It's fine," she said. "I'll be out. You're my first call."

"Thanks, Dr. Anna. I owe you."

He hung up. Nothing sinister in his voice, just annoyance
at his brother.

Anna got herself out of bed, started her coffee brewer,
and stepped into a hot shower. It was her job to make sure
River County's livestock and pets were well taken care of.
Whether she liked their owners or not was a secondary
concern.

She dressed in boots and jeans, glancing with regret at the
muddy and torn dress she'd tossed on her chair. It was
beyond repair.

Anna bolted out the door moments later, stopping only to
fill her travel mug with freshly made coffee.

The old Morgan place, which the Haynes brothers had
taken over, lay on a stretch of highway west of Riverbend.
This was the edge of River County, where the land started to
flatten and the river narrow.

She bumped through the gate to the ranch and down the long, unpaved drive. A one-story house lay to the right, surrounded by mesquite for summer shade. The barn and ranch office were behind the house another dusty half mile.

As Anna had told Kyle, when she visited the Haynes place she usually dealt with the ranch manager, but as she parked her truck and slid out, the lanky man was nowhere in sight.

Half a dozen or so steers lingered in a small muddy corral near the ramshackle barn. At least they'd rounded up the sick ones and separated them, instead of expecting Anna to go out on the range and run them down herself. That happened sometimes.

Of course, these steers were simply roaming around the pen. She saw no squeeze chute, where each animal could be isolated so she could examine it and medicate it without danger to herself.

"Dr. Anna." Jarrod Haynes slouched toward her from the ranch office, hands in his jeans pockets. He wasn't a bad-looking young man, in his early thirties, with brown eyes and sandy blond hair. He hadn't shaved in a couple days, and possibly hadn't changed his shirt since then either.

"Morning," Anna responded as she dragged her heavy medical kit from the bed of her truck. "Where's your manager?"

Jarrod looked around as though surprised, then he rubbed his stubbly chin. "Oh, we canned him. Virgil did, anyway. Said we were paying him too much to do what we could do. Like I said, Virgil is a butthole."

Anna's irritation at the brothers rose. It wasn't like a ranch manager could just turn around and find another job at the same level. Most ranches couldn't pay a lot in any case.

The man might have to move out of the county just to make ends meet.

"These are the steers?" she asked in a neutral voice.

"Yep. Don't really know what's wrong with them."

"Then I'd better take a look."

Jarrod followed Anna closely as she approached the corral. The steers saw her coming, sensed "vet," and shuffled to the far side.

Anna slid the bolt back on the corral's gate, noting that the metal poles were rusty. There was a reason she wore gloves when she worked and made sure her tetanus shot was up to date.

Jarrod hung back, planting himself next to the gate as she entered the corral. He wasn't about to follow her.

Fine with Anna. She closed and latched the gate and approached the steers, making sure her medical bag didn't clink and spook them.

The cattle looked pathetic. When animals were ill, they took on the most dejected, heart-breaking expressions. Eight steers stood in this corral, hooves deep in mud, watching Anna with lack-luster eyes.

No mucus running from noses, though, no open sores that she could see. She approached the smallest one, moving quietly and standing still a while until it decided she wasn't a threat, then she scratched it between the ears.

Another raised its tail and let out a stinky stream. Anna held her breath, the back of her gloved hand to her nose.

"It's scours all right," she said to Jarrod. "Can happen when they're in wet pasture. I'll dose them, but you need to keep them separated for a week or so, so they don't pass the infection to the others. They need to be in a drier corral, and you'll have to clean their feed bins so they don't accidentally eat the infected feces."

Jarrod grimaced and looked worried. "A week? Virgil wanted them turned out today."

"Well, they can't be, or they can infect the entire herd." Anna looked over the cattle, who watched her with dull expressions. "I can explain to him if you want."

Jarrod heaved a sigh. "Nah, it's okay. I'll tell him."

He moved off in the direction of the office, squaring his shoulders as though going into battle. Anna felt a bit sorry for him.

Sure enough, Anna soon heard raised voices from the office. She filled her syringe, turning her back on the steers to hide what she was doing. Animals, like kids, hated getting shots.

She moved among the cattle, thankful Jarrod had left her alone. The young steers were on the small side, and docile enough. She patted them, both to distract and reassure them as she injected the medicine.

All three Haynes brothers emerged from the office. Virgil was the largest and oldest—Anna remembered from school that he'd bullied his younger brothers unmercifully. He bullied those outside his family even harder.

Blake was brother number two, intimidated by Virgil but always striving to prove himself. Jarrod was the nicest of the three, but that was a stretch.

They continued to argue as they halted on the porch, paying no attention to Anna, and she realized after a moment they weren't talking about the cattle.

"You know that truck flipped," Jarrod was saying. "If Sherrie saw the plate, she'll know it was you. Or at least one of us."

"She didn't see anything," Blake snarled. "Stop worrying like a little girl."

Virgil broke in. "Anyone finds out, I'm cutting your balls off. I heard Sherrie was fine and so is the horse, so it doesn't matter. But I'm not paying for her truck."

Anna kept her head bent, eyes on the steer she dosed, but her heart beat faster. A hit and run was a crime, didn't matter that no one was hurt. And who knew if Sherrie was truly all right? She could have damage that hadn't been immediately apparent.

"Hey!" Virgil's voice cut across to the corral. "What is Dr. Anna still doing here?"

"Fixing the steers," Jarrod answered with a growl. "You told me to call her."

"Well, she can finish and go. Get those steers turned out, Jarrod. I'm not paying for feed when they can graze."

"She said they have to stay here a while," Jarrod tried.

"The fuck."

Virgil's boots crunched on gravel as he stormed to the corral. He was a larger version of Jarrod. Blake, behind Virgil, was right in between in size.

"I want them steers out of here, now," Virgil barked at Anna.

The steers moved restlessly, Anna in their midst, but Anna regarded Virgil calmly. Most men were larger than she was, but she'd learned, the hard way, that it wasn't size that counted. If she looked a man in the eye and told him what was what, she usually prevailed.

Even so, she kept the steers between herself and Virgil, who, like Jarrod, remained outside the corral. She idly wondered if Virgil was afraid of his own cattle.

"These guys need to stay separated." Anna slid the syringe

into her pocket, but she remained with the steer, patting him. *My protector.* "Or the rest of your herd could be compromised."

Virgil obviously didn't care. "Now, listen here, angel. You doctor them up and send them off. I can't afford to keep them around all day."

"If you turn these steers out on the range, and your entire herd gets sick, you could lose every single one," Anna said. "Nothing left to sell. Can you afford *that?*"

More scowling. "You don't know what you're talking about, lady."

Anna shrugged. "You can get a second opinion, of course. Call in the vet from Llano. He'll confirm, but he'll charge you a fee for coming out here."

Virgil hesitated. Ranching was a costly business, and Virgil was more penny-pinching than most.

"I think she's right," Jarrod said. "Better have eight die than two hundred."

Virgil reddened as though he wanted to argue, but Jarrod's logic couldn't be disputed.

"All right." Virgil pointed a blunt finger at Anna. "But if you're lying to me and there's nothing wrong with these cattle, I'm suing you for whatever the hell I'm paying you today, and then some."

Anna made it her policy to return her fee if she misdiagnosed, which happened very rarely, but she wasn't going to tell that to Virgil.

"Give her a check, Blake." Virgil gave Anna a final glare and stomped away.

Blake took a checkbook from his pocket, balanced it on the top rail of the corral, and poised a pen over the page. "What's the charge?"

Anna remained with the steer. She expected Blake at any moment to realize she and Kyle could have seen him on the road last night, and try to terrorize her into silence.

But then, Kyle's car had been a rental, not his distinctive truck, and he and Anna would have been an anonymous blur in the dark. From the way Blake had been driving, he hadn't paid much attention to his surroundings.

Anna remained nervous, though. She also sincerely hoped none of them realized she'd overheard their exchange about Sherrie as they'd come out of the office.

"Two hundred and fifty," she said. "That's for the call out and the medication."

Blake stared at her in disbelief. "That's way too much. I'll give you a hundred."

Anna barely stopped herself from rolling her eyes. The medication alone cost her a hundred, and then there was gas, her time, her expertise, and the fact that she had to drive all the way out here and put up with the Haynes brothers.

"Give her the two-fifty, asshole," Jarrod growled.

Blake's eyes narrowed. "What's wrong with you? You in love with her?" He stared at his brother, and then burst out laughing. "Aw man, you stupid shit. All right, I'll give her the whole thing, but it's coming out of your cut."

Jarrod was red-faced. "Fine."

Blake tore out the check, handed it to Jarrod, and walked off, laughing.

Anna gave the steer a final pat, picked up her bag, and headed out of the corral. The steers followed her. That happened often—she was nice to cattle and they started thinking she was their mom. Another reason she couldn't eat beef.

Jarrod handed her the check as she emerged, flapping it a little.

Anna took it between two fingers. The check was dirt-smudged, but that wouldn't matter when she deposited it. "Thanks, Jarrod. It was nice of you to stand up for me."

"Yeah." Jarrod remained beet red, which didn't look good with his unshaved and not very clean face. "Anna. Um—" He cleared his throat then said in a rush, "Will you go out with me?"

Anna stopped. *Shit.*

She felt sorry for Jarrod—who wouldn't?—but that didn't mean she wanted to date him. Far from it. But he looked as pathetic as the steers, so she fumbled for an excuse.

"Oh. I'm sorry, Jarrod, but ..."

"Yeah, I get it." Jarrod looked even more embarrassed, with the beginnings of humiliation. "Don't worry about it."

"No, I mean ..." Anna thought rapidly. "I'm flattered, but I'm already seeing someone. In fact, we're going out tonight."

"You are?" Jarrod sounded amazed, which was kind of insulting, if Anna pondered it closely. "With who?"

"Kyle Malory." Well, it wasn't a lie. Anna still owed him a date. The *tonight* part was the only thing she fudged.

"Really?" Jarrod's humiliation abruptly faded. "One of those Malory shits? Why?"

"Kyle's a nice guy," Anna said, then was surprised by her adamancy.

Jarrod looked Anna up and down in incredulity. "I question your taste, but okay. Kyle was a serious pipsqueak in school."

"Pipsqueak?" Anna had to grin. "Does anyone still say that?"

"It's a good word for him. Virgil and Blake beat him up every day, and he'd run crying to his big brother."

Anna didn't remember Kyle ever crying, and in fact, she'd seen him hold his own time and again against the Haynes bothers. True that Ray would come quickly to Kyle's aid, but Jarrod was wrong that Kyle had wept and wailed. Jarrod either hadn't witnessed the fights or he was varnishing history to make it what he wanted.

Jarrod sent Anna a pitying look, but at least he didn't demand the check back. "Anyway, say hi to him."

Anna slid the check quietly into her pocket. "I will. If the steers keep pooping like that after a couple days, or you notice any of the others with the same symptoms, let me know."

"Sure." Jarrod nodded. Anna hoped he would do what she told him, for the cattle's sake.

It was difficult to leave the steers who watched her mournfully. Jarrod regarded her much the same way. She was glad she'd made him feel better about turning him down, but he still looked morose.

Best thing for Jarrod would be to get himself away from his brothers and live with better people. His life wasn't Anna's business, but she hated to see people unhappy.

She got herself into her truck, waving to Jared, pretending her heart wasn't pounding in both aftershock and relief.

Halfway down the highway to Riverbend, she jabbed a button on her dashboard to turn on her cell phone, and called Kyle.

"About that date I owe you," she said when Kyle picked up and greeted her. "How's tonight?"

Chapter Nine

Not long before Anna called him, Kyle leaned next to his brother at the riding ring, trying to pry information out of him. Never easy, because Ray Malory answered personal questions with a grunt or a glare—when he didn't totally ignore them.

Inside the ring, one of their trainers worked with a new cutting horse. Kyle watched a moment then pushed back his hat and asked casually, "So, who is this Drew?"

Ray gave him a sideways look, a hard one. "I'm sure everyone in the diner told you about her. Why ask me?"

Kyle shrugged, pretending indifference. "Because *you* were the one having dinner with her."

"*You* were having dinner with Dr. Anna," Ray returned. "Believe me, that was way more interesting."

"Everyone knows about Anna's bet with me. But we don't know about you and Drew Paresky."

"See?" Ray turned his gaze back to the rider and horse. "You know her name."

"Anna told me. She treated their cat."

Ray gave him a nod. "Cinders, yeah."

Kyle stared at him. "Cinders?"

"Because we found her in the fireplace."

Kyle planted his booted foot on the bottom rail. "*We?* Okay, so you know their cat's name and you found it with them. While I've never heard about any of this."

"You've been busy. How's Anna?"

Typical Ray, turning the conversation away from himself. "She's fine. What you been up to? Haven't seen you around here much."

Ray scowled. "Have I let the ranch go to shit? No. Then what's the deal? I have my own life."

When Ray was cranky it meant he had something to hide.

"You seeing her?" Kyle asked.

"I can see her—I have eyes. But no, we're not going out or engaged or secretly married." Ray gave Kyle another hard look. "Drew needs to turn around the B&B, and I'm helping her out." He faced the ring, clamping his lips shut.

Kyle started to ask another question—no way he was letting this go—when his cell phone rang.

When he saw Anna's name, he turned away abruptly, Ray and his interesting new hobby forgotten.

"Hey there," Kyle said, hoping he didn't sound too eager. "What's up?"

His pulse jumped as he remembered kissing Anna on the dark porch, imbibing her taste, her strength. She was all kinds of good, and the way she'd clung to him had sent his need rocketing.

She'd be perfect in bed, holding him hard as he thrust inside her, eyes blue and soft in the night ...

"About that date I owe you," she began. Kyle held his

breath, waiting for her to tell him to go to hell, lose himself, fall off another bull and do more damage this time.

"How's tonight?" Anna finished.

Kyle shook the phone. Anna couldn't have just said that. "Tonight?"

"Sure. Anywhere you want. It doesn't have to be Chez Orleans. There's a new place near Johnson City that's supposed to be good ..."

Kyle had no idea what plans he had for tonight. Probably nothing but catch up on TV while he nursed his lingering aches.

"I'll call Chez Orleans and see what they can do," he heard himself say.

"No, no," Anna answered quickly. "They book up months in advance."

"The manager's a fan. Loves the rodeo."

He expected Anna to say something like "Figures," but she only paused and then said, "All right. Want me to drive this time?"

"No, I'll pick you up. Like a real date."

Another hesitation. "Okay. Let me know what time. Thanks, Kyle."

Kyle shook the phone again. "Uh. You're welcome."

"Gotta go. Talk to you soon."

Click. Silence. The phone flashed that the call had ended.

Kyle felt Ray's eyes on him, his older brother crowding his back. "Was that Dr. Anna? What did she want? What did she say?"

Kyle turned as quickly as his healing ribs would let him. "What the hell?"

Ray's lips twitched. "It's a bitch when someone bugs you about *your* personal life, isn't it?"

"Yeah, yeah, all right." Kyle slid the phone thoughtfully into his shirt pocket. "I'm taking Anna out again tonight. Okay? You can tell anyone you want. Including Drew."

He danced back as Ray swung a half-hearted fist. Kyle halted a few feet away, his heart light. "Hey, that didn't hurt at all. I guess I'm getting better."

Ray's eyes glinted. "Keep your mouth shut about Drew and you'll stay that way."

Kyle held up his hands. "All right. I surrender. You tell me about her when you're ready. Right now I need to make some phone calls."

Ray watched him, mouth stubbornly closed, though his face held amusement at Kyle's excitement.

But why shouldn't Kyle be excited? Anna had called him, out of the blue, breathless and eager to go out with him.

Kyle was no fool. He immediately phoned Chez Orleans and had his table from last night booked all over again.

If Anna thought the previous night awkward, it was nothing compared to this one. Last night had been about the bet, and then she and Kyle had helped Sherrie and her horse, putting aside their differences for a common cause.

Tonight was about Anna and Kyle. He picked her up in the same rental car, again in a suit—he apparently owned more than one.

Anna hadn't had time to rush out and buy a new dress, so she put on an older one, a dark pink a few years out of date, but it made her cheeks glow. She'd brushed out her hair and left it down, the all-day braid leaving a crinkle she liked.

Mrs. Kaye again watched as Kyle escorted Anna to the car, the lady waving as they drove off.

The ride down the same dark road toward White Fork was uncomfortably silent. After preliminary *hellos* and *how was your day?* Anna and Kyle didn't speak at all.

She kept her hands bunched in her lap as the shadowy hills went by, the sky a deep twilight. Kyle glanced at her from time to time, but he remained quiet.

Anna preferred the banter from last night, when they couldn't open their mouths without arguing. This was tense and weird.

She cleared her throat when they reached the spot where Sherrie had gone off the road. A few orange cones outlined the shoulder, where Ross and his deputies had investigated the scene. "Hope Blake Haynes isn't out driving again tonight."

Kyle gave her a sharp look. "How'd you know it was Blake?"

"Well ..." With relief that they'd found a topic of conversation, Anna told him about overhearing Virgil threaten Blake if anyone discovered what he'd done. "I called the sheriff's office and told Deputy Harrison what I heard. He noted it but said even with that it might be hard to prove, since we didn't actually witness the accident. So unless Sherrie saw something definite or Blake confesses, he might get away with it. But Harrison will tell Ross."

Kyle kept staring at her, saying nothing.

"What?" she asked after an unnervingly long time. "You think I shouldn't have reported it?"

Kyle jerked the wheel then straightened them out. "Hell yes, you should have. You also should have told me. I'll go out there and take Blake apart until he coughs up the truth."

"Very courageous of you. I don't think it would work, though. You'd have to go through Virgil and probably Jarrod too, and maybe get arrested for assault."

Kyle didn't look worried about any of that. "You sure they don't know you heard them?"

"I have no idea. I think if they did they wouldn't have let me leave so easily. Jarrod asking me out had nothing to do with it—I'm pretty sure."

The car swerved again. *"Jarrod asked you out?"*

"Yes. I turned him down, but I hurt his feelings. I feel bad about that."

"Jarrod Haynes doesn't have any feelings, except selfish ones," Kyle growled. "Wait a sec—is that why you asked *me* out? Because of Jarrod?"

"Kind of. I told him you and I had a date tonight, and I didn't want to make it a lie."

Kyle took his foot off the gas, as though ready to stop the car, then he stomped on it, and they leapt forward. "Crap on a crutch, Anna. Stupid me for thinking you called because you wanted to see me again. But guess what? Too bad for you. I'm not cancelling this. We're going to the damned restaurant, and we'll eat the damned food, and then I'll drive you home, and to hell with you."

"Kyle ..."

"It's what every guy wants to hear. *I'm going out with you so I don't upset another guy.* Thanks a lot, Anna. I'm glad you gave it so much thought."

"But ..."

Anna's words died as Kyle gazed stonily down the road. That was exactly what she'd done—or was it? Part of her had welcomed the excuse to call Kyle for the make-up date.

All right, so most of her had welcomed the excuse. Just

talking to Kyle on the phone had spread agreeable heat through her.

Anna knew exactly what the heat meant. Kyle Malory pushed all the right buttons—good looks, engaging smile, the wicked light in his eyes, and a body that stopped her heart. Women who wanted him weren't fools.

And now she'd pissed him off. No matter what people said about him, Kyle wasn't a mindless rutting machine, plowing any woman who walked in front of him. He was the kind of guy who'd stop at the scene of an accident and help, comforting a shaken woman and her upset horse, who'd ruin a suit doing it and not think anything about it. Who'd give up reservations at a fancy restaurant to accompany the horse to the vet's and then take the tired vet to the diner to make sure she ate.

"Kyle, I'm sorry," she said softly. "I was trying to get Jarrod off my back so I could leave the ranch before his brothers stopped me. I jumped at the first idea that came into my head. But you're right. I should have been straight with you."

Kyle gave her a quick nod. He didn't answer but stared down the road, his lips tight.

Well, she couldn't blame him for staying mad. But how to save the situation?

She grasped at a topic. "So, how's Chocolate and the foal?" She'd kept the mare called Chocolate in her stables not long ago, until the horse, who'd been having difficulty, had successfully given birth.

"They're both fine." Kyle said the words curtly. He snapped his mouth shut again, more silence descending.

"And Ray?" Anna went on nervously. "How's he?"

Kyle shot her another swift glance. "He wouldn't tell me about Drew. I asked."

"I like her." Much easier to gossip about other people than examine what was between—or not between—Anna and Kyle. "She's got a tough row to hoe, but I think she has the stamina to do it. Her daughter, Erica, is twelve, ready to start junior high."

"About the same age as Faith, then."

"We should introduce them, if they haven't met already. They probably have, though Drew is keeping Erica close to home."

Kyle's hands tightened on the wheel, and Anna realized she'd said *we*. As though they were a couple, as though they'd stand hand-in-hand while they welcomed Riverbend's newest resident.

Kyle spoke into the tense silence. "It's a small town. Knowing Faith, she's already leading a crusade to welcome her."

"Faith is warmhearted."

"Yeah, she's a cute kid."

At last, something they could agree on. "Faith really enjoyed following me around that day, helping me. She'll make a good vet, if she decides to go that way."

"She does like animals."

Of course, agreeing on everything meant conversation would run out quickly. "Would be nice to see that B&B up and running again," Anna babbled. "Maybe we'll get visitors who'll want to keep River County as beautiful as it is."

Kyle nodded once. "People do come here to get away from it all. Is that why you came back?"

Awkward again. "Sort of. Nice to be with people I know. I

got tired of the disbelieving looks of ranchers when I showed up to geld their horses or inoculate the cattle."

"Bet you put them in their places."

"I tried to show them I knew what the hell I was doing. But having to prove yourself every single day is exhausting."

"Well, everyone in Riverbend loves you."

He said it with no warmth at all.

The road stretched before them, long and narrow. Even longer would be the dinner coming up at the most romantic restaurant in the county.

Anna gritted her teeth. She'd get through this. She'd eat and smile and try to make conversation until they'd been there long enough to satisfy the bet and the nosy people of Riverbend. Then Kyle would drive her home and never speak to her again.

Chapter Ten

K yle pulled in to the parking lot at Chez Orleans two minutes before the reservation.

The place was packed. Cars and trucks spilled out from the small dirt lot to the grass around it.

In spite of the blow to his ego that Anna had called him only to save herself from Jarrod Haynes, Kyle couldn't help being smug when he opened the door for Anna and walked her inside the restaurant.

She filled out the sexy pink dress she'd chosen and killed it with her shapely legs and high-heeled shoes. Her hair was down tonight, a swath of gold cascading past her shoulders, the silk of it beckoning his touch.

Guys looked at her and let their gazes linger. Women did too, both admiring and envious. There were a few amazed faces as well—*That's Dr. Anna? Whoa, who knew she was such a fox?*

Kyle had always known.

The maître d' was the rodeo fan who'd made sure Kyle could get in tonight. He greeted them and led them to their table, asking Kyle how he was holding up after his fall and which rodeos he'd be riding when he finished healing. Anna, who had obviously thought the fan was a woman, tried and failed to hide her surprise.

The maître d' finally clapped Kyle on the back and left them. Kyle pushed in Anna's chair while a waiter slipped from the shadows and dropped a napkin in her lap.

This place was seriously swank. At least three waiters hovered at each table, one for wine, one for food, one for coordinating the other two. The menu was one page, simple, and not full of weird food that no one really ate except to impress other people.

The chef had stuck to steaks and fresh fish flown in every morning from the Gulf, as well as vegetarian dishes that Anna eyed with approval.

At least the ritual of ordering kept things moving. Anna chose a mixed-leaf salad with goat cheese and fried garlic "chips," and a dish of multi-colored baby carrots in a rich sauce.

Kyle decided, in a fit of what-the-hell, to order vegetarian as well.

"The mushroom thing," he told the waiter. "Sounds good."

Anna blinked at him over the small table when the waiter grinned and glided off. Candlelight sparkled in her very blue eyes.

"You feeling all right?" she asked.

Kyle shrugged. "You said they did vegetarian well here. I thought I'd try it."

"Must be your meds. Did you accidentally take too many?"

"Ha ha. I'm off my meds anyway. Which is great—I've missed beer."

"This is more of a wine place." Anna glanced at the sommelier who uncorked the bottle of pinot noir they'd ordered and trickled wine into her glass. She tasted it and nodded, and the man filled both glasses.

"Notice he gave *you* the taste and not me," Kyle said, amused. He took a sip and pretended to contemplate. "Mmm, I sense … um … wine."

Anna gave him a little smile. "They know you're all about beer."

Kyle stared at the dark red wine—the only glass he'd have since he was driving. "This isn't bad. I guess. I have no clue."

"Doesn't matter. If you like it, drink it. If you don't …" She waved a vague hand. "Don't worry about it. Life's too short to spend it on things you don't like."

"Like Jarrod Haynes?"

Kyle had intended to make her laugh, but Anna flushed. "I really am sorry about that. You're right—I didn't give it much thought."

"I shouldn't have said that. You just smacked me in my pride." He sent her what he hoped was a reassuring grin. "I want to think I'm irresistible."

Anna's flush deepened. "I wouldn't have called if I truly didn't want to go out with you. I'd have called … oh, I don't know. Anyone else." She leaned forward, the soft light making her face more beautiful than ever. "I told Jarrod we were a thing. But don't worry. I won't make you pretend we are."

Kyle hid his edginess by taking another sip of wine. It was smooth, kind of nice. Full-bodied, the sommelier had said. "We can keep this platonic. I forced you into this date in the first place."

Anna was nearly as red as the wine, and also full-bodied.

"I wouldn't say *forced*. I agreed on the bet, and I knew the consequences."

A date with him was a *consequence*? The wine suddenly tasted bitter. But what had Kyle expected? That she'd go starry-eyed and fall in love with him because he took her to a fancy restaurant?

This woman stared bulls in the face and poked them with sharp objects, and they stood there and took it. She'd gone alone to the Haynes ranch without fear—went to a lot of ranches full of guys happy for a visit from a pretty woman—and never had a problem.

"Tell you what, though," Kyle said. "If Jarrod or his brothers try to mess with you, keep on telling them you're with me. I'll go out there and talk some sense into them if I have to. That goes for any ranchers who give you shit."

And for some reason, Kyle had said exactly the wrong thing.

Anna went frosty. "I can do my job," she returned in a hard voice.

Before Kyle could defend himself, the meal was delivered. This place didn't give you dinky salads or salty soups before-hand—you got what you ordered, period.

Kyle's plate held a crock topped with a puffy dough sprin-kled with black pepper. Smelled good even if it looked weird.

"I never said you couldn't do your job," Kyle continued in a low voice after the waiters had backed away. "But some of these guys don't get out much, and they might decide your services include more than doctoring their animals. If they know me and Ray will hand their asses to them if they even look at you wrong, they'll be more respectful."

"I can hold my own, Kyle," Anna said stiffly. "I've been doing it for some time now."

"I know, but guys like the Haynes boys don't care. I'm not saying *you're* incompetent. I'm saying *they're* assholes."

"I know. I'm careful. I'm not a wimpy girl who needs rescuing."

Kyle raised his brows. "Oh yeah? I thought that's what I was doing tonight. Rescuing you from a date with Jarrod."

"Yes, all right. We can argue about that forever. Eat your food."

Kyle poked at the pastry, which easily flaked away. Beneath was a vegetable stew, thick and hearty, smelling of peppers, onions, and fresh herbs. He took a tentative bite, and blinked in surprise.

"Damn—this is *good.*"

"Even if it isn't dead cow?" Anna asked, looking innocent. She took a bite of carrots in silence, but her flickering expression told him she was going to flavor heaven.

Kyle made a conceding gesture. "You're right—they know how to cook vegetarian. This is awesome. I bet my sister could make this if I asked her."

Anna nodded. "Grace is pretty amazing. She might jump at the chance to cook something besides steak night after night."

"It's not steak *every* night." Kyle kept a straight face. "Sometimes she does chicken." He let himself grin. "She makes Carter eat all kinds of stuff. He looks happy enough, so it must be good."

Anna showed a glimmer of a smile. "I think *that* has something to do with more than Grace's cooking."

Kyle flinched. "Nope. This is my *sister* we're talking about. I've reconciled with her being in love with Carter Sullivan, but I don't want to think too much beyond that."

"Why not? Sisters are people too."

"No." Kyle took another bite of the mushroom ambrosia. "They're not, not when they're yours. Brothers either. When they go out into the world, they are people to other people. But to me, they're in this odd place where you love them and want the best for them, and seriously want to lock them in the basement at the same time 'cause they drive you crazy."

"Hm." Anna considered this. "I bet they think the same thing about you."

"They do. Grace especially. She thinks I'm way overprotective."

"Gee, I can't imagine why."

The good food was softening them both, but not quite. The stiffness was still there.

"Because I know guys and how they think," Kyle said. "And some think it's perfectly okay to be total buttheads to women, because women are supposed to be their personal needs-satisfiers. Cooking, cleaning, and … everything else."

"Putting out." Anna took a demure bite of her carrots.

"I was trying to be tactful. So when I see those same guys near my sisters, or near *you*, yeah, I get a little overprotective. And I'm always going to be, so live with it."

Anna only watched him. No agreement, or apology, or understanding. Just looking at him with those gorgeous blue eyes.

Kyle waited for her to growl at him that neither she nor his sisters needed to be taken care of, but damn it—

Anna nodded. "You might have a point."

"I do?" Kyle blinked in surprise. "I mean—"

He broke off as two people stopped at their table.

Karen Marvin smiled down at them in beneficence. She wore a dress clasped across one shoulder with a diamond pin, leaving the other shoulder bare. Karen was ten years older than Kyle, but her body could compete with a twenty-five-year old's. Better, even, because she worked out and knew how to choose clothes to show off the best of her.

Her hair was pulled off her neck and fixed in what Grace had told him was a French braid, affixed with another diamond pin. That was the only jewelry she wore, which had the effect of drawing all eyes to the diamonds.

The cowboy on her arm was a young rodeo hotshot called Deke ... Something. He'd posted online that he had all kinds of sympathy for Kyle taking a fall, and hoped Kyle's age didn't slow down his healing. Well, probably someone had posted this for Deke, as Kyle wasn't sure Deke could spell.

"How do you like the car?" Karen asked Anna without saying hello. "Isn't it gorgeous? I have two."

"It's very nice," Anna said politely. "Comfortable seats."

"The back seat is especially soft." Karen winked at Anna. "And surprisingly large."

Anna turned wine-red again. Deke guffawed. "Plenty of room."

Karen looked in no way embarrassed. In fact, she smiled in delight and stroked Deke's arm. "Deke's more of a truck man."

"Which is why you bought me one, baby." He kissed her cheek.

Anna retained remarkable control of her expression. "Trucks are more practical for me. Though it's nice to have luxury once in a while."

"That's why I told Kyle to rent it," Karen said. "If he was going to take you out, he needed to do it in style. Especially when he said he was bringing you here. The food is *fabulous*."

"Even Kyle thinks so," Anna said without cracking a smile.

"It can't beat Grant Campbell's chili, but it's not bad," Kyle returned, deadpan.

Deke sent Kyle a condescending look. "Well, no one can eat chili forever. Starts to creep up on you after a while." He put his hand on his flat stomach. "I have a ways to go before that, though."

Karen closed her red-nailed hand around Deke's arm. "Let's get to our table, honey. These two are on a *date*."

Deke let his gaze linger on Anna a bit too long. "Yeah, I heard you lost a bet," he said to her, his tone holding sympathy.

Anna bathed him in a radiant smile. "Oh, no, we squared that already. This date's for fun."

Deke looked confused, as though he couldn't figure out why Anna would want to have dinner with Kyle.

Kyle warmed as Anna switched the smile to him. He knew she was bullshitting, but the idea of her leaping to his defense was a fine one. He wanted to kiss her.

And keep kissing her. Sliding the zipper down the back of her silky dress, letting the sleeveless top ease from her shoulders ...

Karen was loving this. She leaned into Deke as she dragged him away. "Enjoy, you two," she called over her shoulder. "Try the salted caramel apple tart. Seriously good."

She sauntered off, and Deke quickened his steps to keep up with her. The maître d' seated them at a table on the other side of the restaurant.

Anna and Kyle stared at each other. Anna's lips twitched hard, her cheeks going pink from holding in the laughter.

Kyle lifted his wine and took a gulp. "Karen really is doing a lot for the community. In spite of her taste in guys."

"That's what everyone says after a conversation with

Karen." Anna gave up fighting and let her smile come. "I don't think she's going out with Deke for his personality."

"What, you didn't like him? I saw you checking him out."

"Oh, he has great *ass*—ets, but he's not my type." Anna swirled the wine in her glass. "I like a guy with less empty air between his ears."

"Yeah, he's not the sharpest knife in the drawer. Except for thinking up ways to call me old and fat without coming out and saying it."

Anna's eyes widened as she looked Kyle up and down. "By no stretch of the imagination are you *old* or *fat*."

"A washed up has-been, that's what he thinks. Now that I'm out of the running, he'll sweep the season this year." Kyle let out a sigh. "Maybe it is time I left it to the younger crowd."

"Fuck him."

Kyle started. "'Scuse me?"

Anna looked at him with intensity, her eyes sparkling. "I said, fuck him. He's far too full of himself, and that karma will backlash on him one day so hard he won't get out of bed." She jabbed her fork gently toward him. "Don't let him keep you from doing what you want to do, what you're good at. You're injured, and that can be depressing, but next season you'll come back just fine. And then Deke will eat his words."

Kyle regarded her in surprise. "You hate bull riding."

"So? That's me. I'm on the bulls' side. But you shouldn't give up what you're good at because some dickhead implies you're finished. I can't tell you how many people have told *me*, not-so-subtly, that I need to pack it in, settle down, learn to knit, and not mess with dangerous animals. To leave it to the men, because I'm only going to get hurt, and it will be my own fault. *Honey.*"

Kyle's lips parted in bewilderment. "But you're a terrific vet. Whenever you leave our ranch, the animals break down and cry. And they all get well. You know what the hell you're doing."

"Yes" The word held quiet confidence, no boasting. "And you know what the hell you're doing with bull riding. Karen's boy toy needles you because he knows you're better than he is and won't get out of his way. It's easy to let people tear down our confidence, to reach the part of us that thinks we're frauds and fears someone will find out."

Kyle picked up his fork and returned to the mushroom stew.

She had a point. Kyle had strived all his life to be as good as Ray at ... You name it. Bull riding, horse training, running the ranch, impressing women. Kyle had won plenty of belts, trophies, and cash in his own right, proving he was good at his sport, but a tiny voice in the back of his mind had always told him he wasn't as good as Ray and never would be.

Ray had never treated Kyle as though he was lesser than him, but Kyle's younger-brother brain didn't always think logically.

"You mean we both have to tell the world to fuck off," Kyle said. "And concentrate on what we do."

"Exactly."

They ate in silence for a while, Kyle digesting her words. Across the room, Karen laughed merrily, Deke's stupid "haw-haw" ringing over her voice.

He must be good in the sack. Only explanation for Karen putting up with him.

Kyle finished his excellent vegetable stew and patted his mouth with his napkin. "Can I ask you a personal question?"

Anna's eyes flickered. "Can I refuse to answer?"

Kyle shrugged. "If you want. Why don't you have a guy following you around like Deke does with Karen? Or did you have someone in San Angelo? That a reason you came back to Riverbend?"

"Why am I single, you mean?" Anna slid her fork through the sauce left from her carrots. "Because guys don't want a woman who runs off at three in the morning to help out a calf or a horse, or a dog that's been hit by a car."

She answered readily, but Kyle sensed there was more to it than that. Many men also didn't like women who were smarter, more successful, and possibly stronger than they were. Anna didn't put up with much shit.

"Why shouldn't women be single if they want to be?" Anna asked, getting pissed off again. "Maybe we've had it with assholes."

Kyle lifted his hands. "I was only curious. You don't talk much about San Angelo."

"It's a dusty town on the edge of West Texas. Some fun stuff to do there, but I mostly worked."

"And put up with assholes?"

"One or two." She looked him full in the eyes. "I promise you, Kyle, I didn't run back to Riverbend after some big drama. No bad breakup, no guy who broke my heart. I went out with exactly three men in five years, and each relationship never lasted longer than a few months. We didn't break up after something dire—we drifted apart and it didn't work out. I also left because I got tired of people giving me a hard time for not choosing small animal work or finding a nice man to marry me—mostly both. Same thing happens to me here, but at least here I have friends, a cute house, a decent income, and good memories."

"Okay." Kyle sat back. "I get it. You do your thing, and you're content with that. This is just me trying to get to know you. The reason I'm surprised you don't have a boyfriend is because you're smart, funny, and seriously gorgeous."

Anna's blue eyes fixed on him in surprise. She took a breath, as though to shoot him a rejoinder, but one of their waiters chose that moment to dart in and remove plates while another slid a dessert card to the table.

"I'll try the salted caramel apple tart," Anna said without looking at the menu.

"Make it two," Kyle said.

The waiter beamed at them, whisked the cards away, and glided off.

Anna leaned across to Kyle, her dress's neckline giving him a tantalizing glimpse of rounded bosom.

"Are you trying to get into my pants?"

Yes. "Because I said you were gorgeous? That's only the truth. Besides, you're wearing a dress."

"Not funny."

"I promise, I can think a woman is pretty without it being a ploy to get her into bed." Kyle could fantasize about it though. He would about Anna all night. "For example, I think Karen is a pretty woman, but no way. She chased me a little when she first moved to Riverbend, and it scared the shit out of me."

"Karen is pretty scary," Anna agreed.

"Doesn't mean she's not attractive, but I do *not* want to go to bed with her. Just because I'm a guy, with active male hormones, doesn't mean I'm a growling Neanderthal chasing women to drag back to my cave. I have other things to do. Ray would never put up with that anyway. He expects me to work on the ranch from time to time."

Anna's hard look softened. "I guess we both have misconceptions about each other. You're supposed to be a drooling Neanderthal, and I'm supposed to be followed by admiring men who want to propose to me."

"Kind of what we were raised to do, right?"

"Fuck us."

Kyle blinked. "Did you just say ..."

"I mean, we should be who we want, no matter what *you* think, and no matter what *I* think? Deal?"

She reached a hand across the table, but before Kyle could take it, the waiter returned with the apple tarts.

The tarts were tiny things, but smothered in great-smelling caramel and topped with a chocolate sculpted doo-dad that started melting when Kyle touched it.

Anna dove right in. "Mmm," she said, her face relaxing into pleasure. "In spite of her fixation with infant cowboys, Karen has great taste in food."

They stopped talking then, ending the tricky conversation to enjoy the dessert. The taste of it pretty much alleviated the bitterness caused by Deke, and by Kyle's boot in his own mouth.

ANNA DIDN'T RELAX AS THEY LEFT THE RESTAURANT. KYLE insisted on bringing the car around so she wouldn't have to walk the ten feet across the parking lot to it, and she waited awkwardly at the door, other patrons giving her knowing looks.

Kyle was moving much better now, Anna noted, with a spring in his step. No more hobbling or growling about his walking stick.

The car slid smoothly to the entrance. Anna thought about Karen's gleeful smile when she'd told Anna the back seat was roomy, and she went hot.

Kyle said nothing as he opened the car door for Anna, and the silence continued as he drove out of the parking lot and started down the road to Riverbend.

At least, in the restaurant, they'd had the food to talk about, plus conversation about Karen, or their career choices. Now they had darkness, an empty road, and the end of their evening together—however that would go.

"Too bad we can't eat food like that all the time," Anna said to break the quiet. Her voice came out scratchy.

"We'd get tired of it." Kyle rested his hands lightly on the wheel. "And overweight."

Anna nodded. "There's that."

"It's a good thing Grace left home. She's such a good cook me and Ray would be enormous by now."

"You two must be starving with no one to make dinner for you." Anna tried to sound teasing.

Kyle shrugged. "Ray grills a decent steak. And my chili isn't too bad."

"Not a vegetable in sight, right?"

"Not usually. But that mushroom thing I had tonight was really good. I think I will ask Grace if she knows how to make it."

"Good."

Words died into darkness. They were groping for light conversation, not wanting to talk about real things. Such as, would they see each other after this? Would they become friends? Or only speak when they ran into each other in passing, or when Anna came to treat the Malorys' animals?

The twenty minutes to Riverbend had never dragged so much—or gone by so fast.

All was quiet when they reached Anna's house. Mrs. Kaye's windows were dark as before, but this time Anna had left her porch light on.

Anna had the car door open as soon as Kyle pulled to a halt. Her hurried *Thanks, Kyle. See you* died away as he turned off the engine and jogged around the car to usher her out and shut the passenger door for her.

He walked her up to the porch. Last night, Kyle had kissed her—or at least responded to Anna's kiss—but it had been dark, and they'd hidden in the shadows. Tonight, the light blazed, illuminating them as though on stage for any passer-by to see.

Anna unlocked her door. She'd left the living room light on as well, Patches snoozing on the armchair. The cat blinked open one eye, regarded Anna sleepily, then closed the eye again.

She should say something, Anna thought in panic. *Well, this is it. Thanks for the nice dinner. Let me know how Chocolate's foal is doing.* Something.

But words stuck in her throat. If Anna said good night, she knew this would be over, and she and Kyle would go back to being … whatever they had been. Acquaintances who argued about the ethics of bull riding, or about whose job was harder and more dangerous. Or not speaking at all.

Kyle said nothing. He looked down at her, his cheekbones stained red.

He was a nice height, not overly tall or bulky, just solid.

He stayed on bulls by balance, skill, and understanding his abilities. Anna knew that now.

He gazed at her with green eyes every girl in Riverbend had wanted upon her. Kyle was much handsomer now than when they'd been teenagers. His body had filled out, his face square, his expression firm with confidence. Faint lines from smiling feathered the corners of his eyes, pale against the tan.

Anna wanted to know if his body was as solid all the way down, if his muscles were as defined as they looked through his tight T-shirts. If he kissed as expertly lying on her couch as he had standing on her porch.

She wanted to know all these things, and she knew that if she said good night now, she never would.

Taking a deep breath, she grabbed Kyle by the lapels of his coat, yanked him into the living room, and slammed the front door.

Chapter Eleven

A nna felt Kyle start, before her heel snagged in the carpet and she stumbled.

Kyle caught her in hard arms. His smile warmed as Anna gaped up at him, then he kissed her.

His mouth was hard, skilled, as kissable as Anna remembered. She steadied herself on him, sliding hands to his hair, finding it warm and silky.

If she broke the kiss, would he say *thanks but no thanks*, back out of the house, and disappear in the night, laughing at her? Maybe.

She'd better keep kissing him, just in case. Anna parted her lips, and Kyle deepened the kiss, opening her mouth, hands strong on her back. He kissed her thoroughly, warming her with the expertise she'd admired last night.

Anna wanted his coat off. She wriggled her hands under it and shoved it over his shoulders. Kyle shrugged it down his arms, letting it fall to the floor.

The thin shirt beneath let her feel the contours of his body, muscles so hard she couldn't make a dent in them.

Kyle's injury might have slowed him down, but it hadn't weakened or softened him.

A tendril of worry broke through Anna's frenzy. "I don't want to hurt you."

Kyle rumbled with laughter. "Damn, Anna. You are the sweetest woman I've ever known."

"No, I'm not. Not sweet. I don't know how to be."

She had no idea what she was babbling. Kyle laughed again. "You're amazing. You can rip off my clothes all you want."

"You too," Anna whispered. "Only—I like this dress."

Kyle's sinful look melted her bones. "I'll be careful."

He had the back zipper down in a swift glide. Her dress, loose, fell from her shoulders, baring her satin bra. She was glad she'd put on the bright thing tonight instead of the sports bra she usually wore.

Kyle gazed down at her in appreciation. He cupped her elbows, eyes half-closing as he leaned to her.

Anna wasn't thinking clearly, but she knew they needed to get out of the living room. She'd closed the curtains before she left, but the wide window gave onto the porch, very close to the street, and they might be silhouetted against the drapes for Riverbend to see.

The bedroom was behind the living room. That meant that all Anna had to do was pull Kyle with her through the door, and the bed was right there, the lamp glowing on the nightstand.

Patches lifted his head from the living room chair to watch them go, yawned, and went back to sleep.

KYLE WANTED TO TAKE THINGS SLOW, BUT *SLOW* WASN'T AN option. He was with Anna, her compact curves snug behind the blue bra, hips filling out matching panties.

He wanted her so bad it was killing him. Kyle hadn't been needy in a while, as both pain and meds had kept him sedated.

He'd woken up when Anna had come to shoe Ray's horse that day. His interest had stirred hard when she'd bent over her forge in her snug jeans, proving he wasn't dead yet.

Now he was wide awake in all senses of the word.

Anna's skin was silken under his hands, her muscles tight from the work she did. The labor hadn't hardened her, though. Her curves, her touch, were all softness.

The bed was only a few steps from the door. Anna had made it cozy with a thick quilt and lots of pillows.

Kyle noted this distractedly as they fell on to it, scattering pillows everywhere. Anna lay beneath him, arms outstretched, her smile warm.

He took a moment to study her—blue eyes, shining hair spilling across the quilt, sweet breasts encased in satin. The moment lengthened before Anna pulled him down to her, parting her lips for a long kiss.

"Caramel," Kyle murmured when they came up for air.

"Hmm?" Her eyes were half-closed, languid.

Kyle licked the corner of her mouth. "From the dessert. You have a little caramel just *there.*" He touched his tongue to the forgotten drop on the crease beside her mouth.

Anna rubbed at her face self-consciously, but Kyle moved her hand. "It's gone. And don't worry. I don't mind sugar-flavored Anna."

Her smile faded. Any minute now she was going to ask

what they thought they were doing, or say they should talk about it first. Kyle's heart was beating fast, his blood hot.

He'd stop this, leave right now if she wanted him to, because he wasn't an asshole, but he hoped to hell she didn't want to stop.

Anna brushed his hair back. She touched his face, skimmed her fingertips over his jaw. No talking, no questions.

She lifted herself, arms going around him while she sought him in a kiss. Kyle smoothed his hand down her side as the kiss continued, no longer questioning or tentative. Their hunger was mutual, and the kiss became devouring.

Anna's foot brushed Kyle's leg, and he realized he wore too many clothes. She was already mostly naked, her legs so great she didn't need stockings on this warm night.

Kyle rose from the bed and half-tore off his shirt, then the T-shirt beneath. His pants slid down with ease once he unzipped them—an advantage dress slacks had over jeans. Shoes wedged off and flung aside, pants kicked after them.

He fell back down to the bed, gathering her into his arms. They kissed again, exploring with touch. Anna skimmed her fingers down Kyle's back to his butt, his thighs, then returned to his neck and hair. She liked his hair, it seemed, as she ruffled it, smiling.

Kyle lifted her hair in his fists, bringing it to his lips. Warm silk touched his face, and he took a moment to enjoy the feel against his cheek.

This was not how Kyle had imagined romancing Anna. He'd envisioned rose petals and soft lighting, champagne and background music.

Reality was the bedroom light on full blast, and silence except for the occasional car passing on this quiet street.

But it didn't seem to matter. This was here and now, and they were together, whatever it meant.

Somehow he got Anna's bra unfastened and off, and she was bare against him. She had gorgeous breasts, round and firm, the tips dusky.

He traced one nipple with his forefinger before he leaned down and ran his tongue around it, the point rising to his mouth. He played there, as Anna's breath came faster, her nipple the softest thing he'd ever had in his mouth.

She grappled with the waistband of his underwear, and Kyle decided it was time to make it disappear. He slid the boxer briefs down his legs, kicking them off his feet.

There. Exposed.

Anna studied him with flattering intensity before she wrapped her hand around his cock. Kyle dragged in a breath, the spike of pleasure acute.

"Let's," Anna whispered.

Kyle nodded readily. Only … He hadn't really expected the evening to lead this far.

"Nightstand," Anna said, understanding. "In the drawer."

With a blink, Kyle rolled over and slid open the drawer next to the bed. Inside was a small box of condoms, neat and unopened.

"You're prepared," Kyle said with a grin.

"Callie bought them for me." Anna sounded shy. "When she heard about the bet."

Kyle stifled a laugh. Callie was full of surprises. He opened the box and turned back to find Anna's panties falling from her fingers to the floor beside the bed.

He could only gape like a fool, the wrapped condom he'd extracted dangling from his hand. A swirl of blond hair decorated the space between her legs, her belly curving sweetly.

"Do you know how beautiful you are?" he asked, his mouth dry.

She flushed. "You already know how hot *you* are, so I'm not going to say."

Kyle's blood burned. Beautiful and unique Anna thought *he* was hot. He'd walk on air about that a long time.

He tore open the packet with comical rapidity and slammed the condom over his very ready cock. Anna rose on one elbow, sexy as hell, watching him.

Everything stopped when Kyle came over her. Everything he was and had been was finished. What he'd be after this would be entirely new.

Anna reached for him and welcomed him in.

KYLE WAS A WARM, FIRM WEIGHT, FILLING HER LIKE HE belonged inside her and always had. Anna touched him, couldn't stop, loving the tightness of his body. He braced himself on his fists as he thrust into her, his eyes darkening.

"Sweet," he groaned. "Sweet Anna."

He wasn't going to be a quiet lover. That was fine. Anna didn't think she'd be able to hold back on the noise herself as a wave of pleasure lifted her.

"You're tight." Kyle's voice licked her senses. "So beautiful and tight. *Damn.*"

He stilled a moment, closing his eyes as though absorbing the feeling. When he opened his eyes again, the green in them sparkled. His lazy smile spread across his face, Kyle the rodeo hero back in action.

He slid partway out and inside again. "Oh, yeah."

She rose to meet him. He filled her satisfyingly, pressing her open. A big man, but gentle. His thrusts were about pleasure for both of them, not simply taking what he wanted.

Kyle groaned again, face softening as he relaxed into his rhythm.

"You are amazing," he said, eyes on her. "Amazing, sweet Anna. Fuck, you are good."

Anna wanted to say he was wonderful, hard, hot, and to *keep doing that*, but all that came out was a wordless sound, then breathy gasps, then his name. Her thoughts scattered on a wash of crazed sensation.

Kyle sped his thrusts, his breathing fast. The bright light let her see his gorgeous face, eyes, smile, the trickle of perspiration that ran from his temple to be lost on his cheek.

"Anna." His voice was more urgent. "Shit."

His words tangled and slid away. Anna met him as he came down on her, their groans and cries mingling as she sailed on a wave of joy.

Hard, harder. Anna might have shouted the words—she wasn't sure. Kyle complied. Then they were laughing, moaning, shouting, caught in a whirlwind of dark release.

Anna wasn't certain when it ended, or if it did. They fell together to the mattress, wrapped in each other. Touching, kissing, murmuring. More kissing, hot afterglow.

"Kyle," Anna whispered a final time and touched his face.

"Anna. You are the most beautiful—"

Kyle's words were lost as a flood of sleep washed over Anna, and she dropped into its warm depths without a struggle.

A LOAD OF BRICKS LANDED ON KYLE'S ANKLES AND YANKED
him out of sound sleep. The load squirmed, stabbed him
with ten small knives, and then collapsed onto his feet and
started to purr.

Kyle groaned softly, moved a leg, and was rewarded by
being stabbed again. The purrs grew louder.

He pried open his eyes to see the green ones of a black
and white cat staring at him. Not glaring, not gazing … staring. Assessing. Sizing him up.

Kyle took stock of his situation. He lay face down on
Anna's bed, not wearing a stitch. Anna, sleeping peacefully
next to him, had managed to slide under a sheet, her head
resting on a soft pillow. Her breasts moved the sheet as she
breathed, face relaxed in slumber.

Kyle returned the cat's stare and touched his finger to his
lips. "Let her sleep," he whispered.

The cat watched him serenely. Kyle moved the slightest
bit, trying to find a more comfortable position, and the cat
pounced on his ankles again. Kyle flinched and stifled a
shriek.

Anna opened her eyes. She took in Kyle, his face tight
with pain, his naked body on her bed, and her cat on his
ankles.

Her smile made being wakened by miniature torture
worth it. Anna's eyes lit, and her body shook agreeably with
laughter.

"Patches likes you," Anna said. "He doesn't attack just
anyone's ankles."

"Great." Kyle tried to slide his leg out from under the cat,
but Patches decided he didn't want it to go. He pounced
again, and Kyle yelped.

Anna, laughing her ass off at him, rolled out of bed. Kyle ceased moving to look at her standing in the sunshine.

Silken hair straggled across her shoulders and down to her breasts, which were petite but gorgeous, like the rest of her. Her body, honed by work and exercise, curved in the best places, her arms and neck tanned from the Texas sun. The rest of her was pale, meaning she didn't have time to sit out and bake herself in a bathing suit.

She looked great as she was. Kyle fixed the sight of her in his mind, wanting to remember her like this, uninhibited, laughing in true enjoyment.

"I'm hitting the shower," she said. Kyle loved that she didn't cower, try to cover herself, deny that anything had happened, or shout at him to get out. "I don't have much to offer for breakfast, but I'm seriously good at working the toaster."

"I'm not bad at it myself," Kyle said. "If you have eggs, I can make you a mean omelet. Unless you don't eat eggs, Dr. Vegetarian."

"I will. As long as they're free-range—true free range—and the chickens are happy. That's what kind of eggs you'll find in my fridge, so cook away."

"Sounds good. I've taken over breakfast at home. Unless it's meat outside on a grill, Ray's cooking sucks."

Anna grinned at him and disappeared into the bathroom.

Kyle had a serious talk with the cat. He made Patches a bargain—he'd find the kibbles and fill his bowl if Patches would let Kyle get off the bed without grabbing his feet.

Patches didn't keep his part of the bargain, but by the time Kyle finally got his legs off the bed, the cat had fled, probably waiting for Kyle to uphold *his* end of the deal.

The shower was running. Kyle toyed with the idea of

joining Anna, spreading soap over her, lifting her against the
wall, sliding deep inside her ...

He shook off the vision and willed his cock to calm down.
He had no idea what kind of reception Anna would give him
if he cornered her in the shower. Anna so far didn't seem to
regret their night together—if an hour of hard banging
followed by comatose slumber could be called a night
together.

Kyle turned off the vision, gathered up his clothes, and
pulled them on. He hoped the suit coat would hide the fact
that most of the buttons had been ripped from his shirt.

He went out to the kitchen in his bare feet, found the bag
of cat food, and satisfied Patches by pouring some into
his bowl.

Patches wrapped his tail around the ankles he'd abused
and fell to eating with gusto. Kyle moved back through the
house to the front room, cautiously opening the curtains to
let in the sunlight and the neighbors' curiosity.

He stared outside. "Aw, *shit.*"

The cat came running, but the shower continued to
patter, Anna oblivious to his anguished cry.

The car, the rented luxury Lexus, had vanished. Kyle
yanked open Anna's front door and dashed onto the porch,
but the spot where the car had been parked was empty, the
hideously expensive car gone.

Chapter Twelve

Kyle did make a mean omelet, Anna discovered when she emerged to the smell of frying eggs. She dressed quickly in shirt and jeans and then went out and worked the toaster like a boss to supplement the meal.

She ate with Kyle across the table from her, looking delectable in his rumpled suit and ruined shirt. In spite of the fact that someone had stolen his car, he lingered over breakfast instead of rushing off in panic.

He'd go anytime. And this would be over.

Whatever *this* was.

Anna thought back to the bright day she'd been shoeing Ray's horse and realized Kyle was checking out her ass. She'd yelled at him for it, unable to admit to herself that being the focus of his attention melted her. Her snarling and growling had been at herself for being entranced by Kyle.

He wasn't the same as the guys who'd followed her in college with only one thing on their minds. Kyle looked into her eyes, had conversations with her, didn't expect her to have sex with him in gratitude simply because he'd spoken to her.

When he'd fallen from the bull, Anna had experienced a moment of deep panic, worried he'd broken his neck, killed himself right there in the mud. Helping him walk from the ring had made her light on her feet, rejoicing he was all right.

It could have been so much worse.

Anna shoved her worries aside. "Can I drive you somewhere?" she asked, keeping her voice light. "Home? Sheriff's department? Rental car place?"

Kyle shook his head. "Don't go out of your way. I already called Deputy Harrison and reported the car stolen. I'll walk to the feed store, and Ray can get off his ass and pick me up there."

"You sure? Your ranch is on the way to my office."

My, they were polite this morning.

"Nah, less gossip if I slip out the back."

"Because you walking through the alley and into the feed store in your messed-up suit will cause *less* gossip."

"Good point." Kyle shoveled in the last of his eggs. "But better than walking out your front door with a street full of neighbors waiting for me. At least with the car gone, they might think I left last night and didn't stay over. If I go out the back, it will help reinforce that idea."

Anna finished the last bite of the terrific omelet and laid down her fork. "Kyle, I don't care if they know. But if you want to slip out through the alley I won't stop you."

Maybe he didn't want anyone to know he'd slept with her? Anna wasn't his usual type.

Kyle looked puzzled. "Just trying to save you some embarrassment. The town will find out sooner or later, but

I'm not going to advertise by walking out and waving at everyone. None of their damned business."

Anna shrugged, as though she didn't care. "All right."

Kyle frowned while Anna picked up her toast and munched it. When she said nothing more, he rose and took his dishes to the sink. He even rinsed them off and put them into her dishwasher, along with the frying pan he'd used for the eggs.

Anna was still chewing when he turned back to the table and caught up his cell phone. He didn't leave, didn't call anyone, only stood there as though waiting for her to say something.

Anna laid down the crust and cleared her throat. "So, see you around?" she said.

Kyle waited another heartbeat then smoothed out his face. "Yeah, I guess you will."

He stared down at her for a few more seconds before he stooped and pressed a brief kiss to her lips. "Congratulations, Anna. You paid off our bet."

Another kiss to the top of her head then Kyle breezed out the back door in his usual saunter.

Wind caught the door and banged it closed. The sound was hollow.

Patches leapt to the table and bent an eye on the crumbs on Anna's plate. Instead of shooing him off, Anna stroked him absently.

"I'm really bad at people, aren't I?" she said tiredly. "Especially male people. I suck at it." Anna slid her fingers through the cat's warm fur. "Any advice? Or should I just hunker down and go back to work?"

Patches half closed his eyes, purrs swaying his body.

Anna let out a heavy sigh. "Yeah. Thought so."

HALFWAY TO THE FEED STORE, KYLE'S PHONE RANG.

He found it hilarious how fast he grabbed it. Was it Anna, calling him to come back? Begging him to stay another night? Move in? Lie around all day with her in a naked sex-fest?

It was the guy at the car rental place in White Fork. Kyle let out his breath and answered.

"Hey, look, I'm sorry ..."

"Kyle?" the man talked right through him. "I don't understand. The sheriff's office called me about the car I rented you being stolen, but it's right here. Was at the gate when I opened up. Thanks for dropping it off so early. I think the deputies got their wires crossed."

"What? Oh, yeah. Right. Uh ... Sorry for the confusion."

"No problem. Did you like the car? Have any trouble with it?"

Kyle assured him that the car was wonderful, and no, he didn't know it was for sale, and no he didn't want to buy it. He finally managed to hang up, and then called Ray.

No answer.

Shit.

Kyle went to the feed store anyway. Chances were good he'd find someone there to catch a ride with.

The feed store was in truth the hardware store on the corner of the town square with a big tack and feed shop behind it. Everything a rancher needed was in that store, which had been run by the Fuller family for generations.

Today Mr. Fuller stood behind the counter while his sons and sons-in-law restocked shelves, helped customers, and drove forklifts laden with bags of feed and garden soil.

"Morning, Kyle," Fuller said, looking him up and down with amusement. "Going to a wedding? Might want to change your shirt."

Several of the younger generation Fullers glanced over and grinned. The whole town must know Kyle and Anna had gone out last night, and here was Kyle still in his date-night suit, which was the worse for being half torn off him.

Damn it, Ray.

"She threw me out," Kyle said in a joking tone. "I've been wandering the streets. Any of you making a delivery out my way? Or seen my obnoxious brother?"

Craig Fuller, a friend from way back, shoved a crate onto a shelf and strolled over. "Ray's been spending a lot of time at the B&B old man Paresky left. And a lot of time with its new owner. Can't blame him. She's something good looking."

"A lot of time," Kyle agreed, though his irritation grew. "He won't talk about it. Highly suspicious."

"I know, right?" Craig chuckled.

"Can I catch a ride with any of you?" Kyle steered the conversation back to what he needed.

Craig adjusted his cap that said "Fuller's Feed" on it. "Not anytime soon. Let me check with my brothers …"

"We're going your way." A new voice rumbled behind Kyle, and he grimaced. "Want a ride?"

Kyle turned with reluctance. Craig, the shit, took one look and suddenly remembered he had boxes to move somewhere in the back. Craig was a nice guy, but he was no match for the Haynes brothers and he knew it.

Two of the three Hayneses, Jarrod and Blake, had entered the feed store. Wonderful. At least Virgil wasn't with them—he was probably off torturing innocent souls with his pitchfork.

Blake had been the one who'd spoken. Jarrod gave Kyle a silent once-over, a sullen look on his face.

Kyle rubbed his hair as though considering. "Thanks, but think I'll take my chances hitching."

"Nah," Blake said with a wolfish smile. "We'll throw you in the back and shove you out at your gate."

He would, literally.

"That's okay." Kyle kept his voice neutral. "I'd rather keep my suit clean. I've seen the state of your truck."

"It's new," Jarrod snapped. "Too good for you, Kyle."

Blake rolled his eyes. "Shut up, Jarrod. So, Dr. Anna, huh?" he continued. "Jarrod told me you were *in* her. Wait, I mean, *into* her."

Kyle went cool. "And now we're touching on stuff that's none of your business."

"Better watch her, Malory. She knows her way around a castration knife."

"I'm aware of that," Kyle answered. If Blake shut up and didn't continue down this road, everything would be fine. "Good seeing you, Haynes."

"You hate seeing me, but that's fine. Fuller—I need horse pellets. Alfalfa. Couple of bags. Dr. Anna was out at our place yesterday," he went on as Fuller departed to fill Blake's order. "Sweet woman. *Real* sweet, to all three of us."

Kyle fought for patience. "Now, this is where you and I go wrong, Blake. You can't let it go. You disrespect a woman and needle me until I want to rip off your face and feed it to you. Best you buy what you came here for and take off."

Blake grinned. "Am I getting under your skin? Why's that? Same reason you're walking around in your fancy clothes at eight in the morning? You and Anna did the dirty all night, didn't you? So, tell us—does she do it doggy style? You know, like horses? And dogs?"

"Can you be any more disgusting?" Kyle demanded, tamping down his fury. He'd learned it was best not to let on that Blake was getting to him. "Oh, wait, you can. I've known you a while." He took a step toward Blake. "Tell you what— you leave off talking about Anna—forever—and I'll let you keep your blood inside your body."

Blake, for all his idiocy, hadn't come to fight today. His grin widened and he lifted his hands. "Man, you're in love with her, ain't you? Better you than me, dude. When she cuts off your dick, I'm gonna laugh."

"Seriously, Blake. Don't talk about her again." Kyle kept his stare even. Blake blinked in surprise but registered the threat in Kyle's eyes.

"Whatever," he said. "Come on, Fuller, what the hell is taking you so long?"

Kyle relaxed a fraction, though he wouldn't entirely until these shits drove away. Blake for now lost interest and started after Fuller.

Kyle felt hot breath on his neck and turned to see Jarrod next to him.

Jarrod was a year younger than Kyle and had always let his older brothers fight the Malorys when they clashed. Jarrod, after he'd instigated a fight, would watch from a safe distance. He was fiercely loyal to his brothers, though Kyle wasn't sure why—they gave him all kinds of hell.

"Don't mess with me, Jarrod," Kyle said, tight-lipped. "I'm not in the mood."

Jarrod's eyes narrowed. "You tell Dr. Anna that when you dump her, she can come to me, but I won't be as nice as before. And you can tell her she's a stupid cun—"

Kyle didn't let him finish the word. He had his hand on the back of Jarrod's neck and was marching him out of the store, the final *T* sound ending in a gurgle.

"What the fuck?" Blake roared from the depths of the shelves, but Kyle didn't stop.

He kept Jarrod in a fierce grip until he threw him against the side of a sleek pickup, the one that had passed him and Anna like a bat out of hell two nights ago.

Jarrod landed hard but sprang upright again, his face flinty. Kyle stepped close to him.

"You mess with Anna or even *talk* to her, there's not going to be much of you left. And if you ever use that word about her again, I'm going to move your mouth to the other side of your face. You get me?"

"You want to leave my brother alone, Malory?"

Blake's hand landed on Kyle's shoulder. This was how it had gone down all Kyle's young life. Jarrod would piss off Kyle until Kyle had to threaten him, and then Blake and Virgil would jump in with their fists.

Blake was here without Virgil today, and this wasn't high school, but Blake was a hard man, strong from riding and ranching. Unfortunately for Blake, so was Kyle.

Kyle removed Blake's hand from his shoulder with a forceful grip. "Tell Jarrod to keep his foul mouth shut about Anna. Yours too. You mess with her, you mess with me."

"That so?" Blake Haynes, master of the comeback. "How about you mess with my fist?"

"I can do that." Kyle would have to take the restricting suit coat off to fight, and he wasn't certain Blake would give him time. It was why suits were stupid.

"Heard you were laid up," Blake went on. "I don't want to hurt you."

"Healed." Kyle said, hoping so. His ribs hadn't ached at all last night with Anna, though he wasn't sure he could have felt anything but her, no matter what.

"Let's find out." Blake balled up his hand and delivered a hard punch right at Kyle's ribs.

Chapter Thirteen

Kyle anticipated Blake's punch and blocked, so the blow was not as bad, but it still connected. He grunted and bent over, the breath going out of him.

He heard Jarrod's hyena-like laugh, and then Jarrod's ham fist was coming at Kyle's face. Kyle blocked that blow too, but it gave Blake the opportunity for a kidney punch.

Kyle staggered, knowing he was going down. He'd be on his knees in in the muddy lot, and Jarrod and Blake would kick the hell out of him, or run him over. Or both.

He struggled to stay upright and landed a good smack on Jarrod's jaw before Blake hit Kyle again. Kyle grunted, tasting blood.

"You boys take that out of my parking lot," Fuller yelled behind them. "Or I'm calling the sheriff!"

A fleeting glance showed Fuller standing in the back doorway of the feed barn, threatening them with a cell phone. Craig stood next to him, looking worried.

"Yeah?" Blake jabbed Kyle in the ribs again. "Bring on baby sheriff, Ross Campbell, and his—" He proceeded to call deputies Harrison and Sanchez names that could get him killed.

Kyle was happy to do the deed for them. He elbowed Blake in the gut, hearing a satisfying *Oof!* But Kyle was too winded to follow through, and Jarrod slammed Kyle up the side of the head.

Blake ground out a laugh as he gave Kyle another blow in his lower back. Pain radiated from the base of Kyle's spine, and he heard his coat rip before Jarrod kicked his feet out from under him. Kyle landed on one knee, seeing Blake's foot in a giant boot coming at him.

The kick never landed. A deep-voiced shout came from behind him, and Blake and Jarrod suddenly vanished. Kyle heard Blake's pickup starting and he scrambled away from it, knowing they'd think nothing of running him down.

He climbed to his feet to see Jarrod in the driver's seat, the truck squealing through the parking lot, Blake climbing hurriedly into the pickup's bed. Ray stood beside Kyle, tall and formidable, glaring in fury.

Blake looked over the truck bed, his face a bloody mess, but he managed a laugh as Jarrod pulled onto the street.

"Still need Ray to save you, Malory. Just like—"

The rest of his words were lost as the truck roared around the corner and out of sight.

Ray steadied Kyle with hard hands on his shoulders. "You okay? You look like shit."

"He was trying to say 'just like high school.'" Kyle wiped his mouth, his hand coming away red. "And all the times you helped me kick their asses." He gave his brother a grateful look. "Thanks, Ray."

ANNA HEADED EAST OF TOWN THAT MORNING FOR HER FIRST
call, the temporary home of Callie Jones's rehab ranch.

She drove in a daze. Her body felt new and raw, tender
where she had connected with Kyle.

Her thoughts filled with his smile, his laughter, the way
he groaned her name, his touch, the weight of him on her
body. His kiss as he left her, slipping out the back to save her
from discomfiture.

Good thing there wasn't much traffic, because Anna's
attention was everywhere but on the road. She was never
sure exactly how she'd reached her destination, but the sign
for the Jones ranch loomed suddenly, and she had to slam on
the brakes before she missed it. She skidded in through the
gate, hoping no one had seen her graceless arrival.

Callie Jones, Anna's best friend, had recently married
Ross, the interim sheriff. Callie had added helping Ross
campaign to be elected sheriff to her already heavy workload
—she'd opened a ranch with her friend Nicole to rehabilitate
abused or abandoned horses. Anna had volunteered to
donate her time and expertise as a vet to the venture, which
had helped Callie obtain a start-up grant.

The ranch was doing well so far, except they didn't have a
permanent home. They'd set up in a corner of Callie's dad's
vast estate, but Callie and Nicole wanted a place of their own
where they could spread out if need be.

Already Callie and Anna were treating horses rescued
from abusive or neglectful owners as well as a few coming
off the quarter-horse race tracks, half-crazed and full of
illegal meds.

Anna parked in the small dirt area filled with cars and
horse trailers and hopped out unsteadily.

She found Callie and Nicole in what were called mare

pens—stalls about ten feet square built of corral poles, each with a corrugated metal shelter, feed bin, and water. The setup allowed airflow in the hot climate and also let the horses see each other, which was important for animals that naturally ran in herds.

"Anna!" Callie caught her in a hug. "We need to talk."

"About what?" Anna glanced around in alarm, fearing the horses she'd treated would be falling down in agony. Instead she saw a mare and a gelding pulling at hay in their racks, turning to see who the newcomer was. All tranquil.

Callie laughed. "I mean girl talk. Let's work and then go get coffee."

Anna followed her in uneasiness, wondering how thoroughly Callie would interrogate her. What she had with Kyle was too new, too strange for discussion over beverages.

She forced her mind to the tasks at hand, to check the gelding who'd had such a bad case of thrush she feared she'd have to amputate his hoof, and the half-starved mare who'd proved to be in foal. Anna, Callie, and Nicole had worked hard medicating, feeding, and comforting, and now all the horses were looking much happier. The mare would foal in a few months.

"Hey, Dr. Anna!" a friendly voice sang out.

Manny Judd, the lanky young man Callie had hired to more or less manage the non-medical care of the horses, leaned on a rake and gave Anna a wave. Manny led the team of stable hands with cheerful enthusiasm, grooming, mucking stalls, and keeping straight the feeding schedule and which horses got what. Manny had proved to have a knack for horses, understanding when they needed help.

"Manny," Anna moved to him. "How are things?"

"Around here? Just fine. I'm loving my job. Callie is so

cool." He bent his head as though imparting secrets, but his voice remained at full volume. "I'm going out with Tracy Harrison. Did you know that?"

Anna gave him a conspiratorial wink. Tracy was Deputy Harrison's younger sister, who would be a senior in high school this year. She was pretty and smart, and seemed taken with Manny.

"I've seen you two around. How does her brother feel about that?"

"He's actually cool with it." Manny looked surprised but pleased. "I was terrified about dating a deputy's sister, since he'd know how many times I got myself arrested when I was younger. But Ross and Callie put in good words for me, and Harrison's a pretty reasonable guy."

"I'm glad for you." Anna patted Manny's formidable arm. Manny had once upon a time been a big screw-up, but Callie's generosity in giving him this job, plus dating a young woman who liked him had given him a boost in confidence.

Manny's look turned wise. "So you and Kyle Malory. How's that going? He pop the question yet?"

Anna's face scalded. "Pop the question? Geez, Manny, we've only gone out once. Okay, twice, but the first time didn't count."

Manny spread his hands. "Hey, don't bite my head off. I'm only asking. Every time he's with you, he looks like someone hit him between the eyes. I think it's *love*." He trailed off with a chuckle.

"No, I think it's *Anna lost a bet*. Kyle took me out, that's all. No love, no question popping, no relationship."

Manny listened with a grin. "Sure, Anna. That's why he went in your front door last night and out the back this morning."

Anna gaped at him, then she pressed her hand to her forehead and groaned. "Damn it, I hate this town."

"You can't help it if you live next door to Mrs. Kaye. She was in the diner this morning, telling people all about it. I had breakfast there, which is how I heard. If you want to keep it secret, I won't tell nobody. Though I think it's too late."

"Shit," Anna whispered.

"So, Kyle spent the night with you. From the way you're blushing, I bet he didn't sleep on the couch."

"That's personal," Anna snapped.

"You asking me how Deputy Harrison feels about me going out with his sister is too," Manny said in a reasonable voice. "Just because you're a few years older than me doesn't make it less personal."

He had a point, and Anna knew it. "I'm sorry," she said stiffly. "I just— It's … complicated."

Manny gave her an understanding nod. "It's hard to be in love. But really nice too. Well, I gots to get back to work. See you, Dr. Anna."

"See you, Manny," Anna said faintly. Manny picked up his rake and strode away, whistling.

Love. No. Not love. Manny was a kid, and he didn't understand.

Anna and Kyle weren't in love. They were barely friends. They'd argued, she'd lost, and then they'd had fantastic sex and a wonderful breakfast together. Not love.

So why couldn't Anna stop thinking about Kyle? Planning what she'd say to him next time she saw him? Reliving every kiss, every touch, whisper, smile, and word from the time he'd picked her up last night to when he'd walked away down the alley, the suit coat brushing his fine ass?

She groaned again. She'd have buried her face in her hands if they weren't in gloves covered with dirt, horsehair, and possibly shit.

She settled for gently banging her head against the metal post of the corral. The mare inside eyed Anna curiously, breathing warmth into her face that felt like sympathy.

ANNA AND CALLIE HAD COFFEE AT THE LITTLE BAKERY THAT Grace Sullivan had just opened on the square across from the courthouse. It would be a catering business mostly, but there was space for a few tables so people could drop by for coffee or tea and Grace's amazing pastries.

Already it was a popular place. Late September was still plenty warm in the Hill Country so Grace had put tables on the sidewalk. Callie and Anna took one, with Callie darting inside to purchase the coffee and hunk of cake Grace called a *gateau* covered with whipped cream. Callie insisted on treating.

"I need to tell you everyone's talking." Callie took a bite of the cake, cream smearing her lips. She stopped, closing her eyes. "Oh, I think that's the best thing I've ever chewed."

"Grace knows what she's doing." Anna took a bite and also savored, though Callie's first statement made her too nervous to fully appreciate the cake. "What do you mean, *everyone's talking?*"

"They are. There hasn't been anything new and exciting to talk about in Riverbend since the sheriff got fired and Ross and I married. And then you bet Kyle you could ride the mechanical bull, and you two went to the diner, and Karen saw you at Chez Orleans last night. Karen thinks it's marvelous."

Anna huffed an aggrieved breath. "Like I said to Manny, there's nothing to talk about. Yes, Kyle spent the night—I won't be able to deny that—but he went home alone this morning. End of story."

"Uh-huh." Callie took another big bite of cream. "And then Polly at the counter in there—" She pointed her fork toward the interior of the shop—"told me that Kyle got into a fight with Jarrod Haynes this morning at the feed store, because Jarrod was badmouthing you. Craig Fuller came in for coffee and donuts and told her."

Anna stared, her heart beating faster. "Crap."

Callie nodded. "Punching and everything. Blake jumped in, and Craig thought they'd have to call the police and an ambulance. But Ray came along in the nick of time and Blake and Jarrod high-tailed it out of there."

Anna listened in alarm, lips parting. "Is Kyle all right?"

"Apparently."

Anna's hands shook. "I should call him, make sure he's okay." She looked at Callie in worry. "Should I call him?"

"A show of concern is never unwelcome," Callie said, her voice gentle.

"But me all over him would be … smothering." Anna took an extra-large bite of cake.

Callie laid down her fork. "Let me put it this way—what happens if everyone in town asks if he's all right and *you* don't? How will he feel about that?"

Anna deflated. "I can't win either way, can I?"

"Nope. Not with guys you're into."

"I'm not *into* him. I'm …"

"Yes?" Callie raised her brows as she sipped coffee. "You glad I gave you my little gift?"

"Yes," Anna said mournfully.

Callie's eyes crinkled with mirth. "I thought they'd come in handy. I saw the way you were looking at him. And he at you. *I* bought them because everyone would assume they were for me and Ross." She looked coy.

"It's different. You're married."

Callie's laughter surged. "So? I know, I know—it's less embarrassing, and we really don't need the condoms. If I get pregnant, it doesn't matter. In fact, it will be great. But we're waiting to see what happens with the election."

She finished with confidence, but Anna saw the longing in her eyes, the wistfulness.

"Callie." Anna set aside her own confusion. "I've been your friend forever. No matter when you and Ross have a kid, you'll be deliriously happy. You don't need to wait. You both want children. I can see that."

"I know, but …"

"If you were flat broke or struggling with life I could understand. But he's the beloved Ross Campbell, and you're Callie Jones. Any kid of yours will have it made. They will have loving parents, doting grandparents, indulgent aunts and uncles, and me, your soppy best friend."

Callie's smile died. "I don't want to distract Ross right now. Winning the election is important to him. And him running for sheriff was kind of my idea."

"He wouldn't have gone for it if he hadn't truly wanted to." Anna reached for Callie's hand. "Trust me, if you leave off the condoms and have a baby, he will be all kinds of thrilled. *And* he'll be sheriff."

Callie squeezed her fingers. "I'm supposed to be giving *you* advice."

"I know, but it's much less pressure on me when it's the other way around."

Callie slid her hand from Anna's and pointed at her phone. "Call Kyle."

"I will. I'll …"

"I mean right now." Callie's finger twitched. "Pick it up. I'm sure his number is already in there. If not, I'll call Grace and—"

"All right. All right." Anna hurriedly lifted her phone.

Of course Kyle was already in her contacts. She'd made him his own entry so the screen said *Kyle* when she touched it.

He picked up after the third ring. "Anna?" The word was wary.

Anna swallowed the huge lump in her throat. "Hi. I, um …"

Callie mouthed, *Wanted to see if you were doing okay.*

"I wanted to see if you were doing okay," Anna repeated. "Callie said you might have, um, gotten hurt."

Callie gave her a thumbs-up.

"I'm fine," Kyle said stiffly. "Nothing serious."

"Good. Good." Anna drew a breath. "They didn't, I mean …"

Callie shook her head vigorously, making slashing motions with her finger over her throat.

"Didn't what?" Kyle asked. "Are *you* all right?"

"Nothing. I'm fine." Anna clenched her hand in her lap. "Well, if you need anything, give me a call."

Kyle's voice softened. "I'll do that. You have a good day."

"You too. See you, Kyle."

"Take care, Anna."

He finished with *Bye-bye, now,* in his deep Texas drawl, and Anna flushed and hung up.

"Perfect." Callie grinned and lifted her coffee in salute. "Perfect. Second date, with more condoms, is assured."

Anna wasn't certain she could grow any hotter. "I wasn't trying—"

Her phone rang, and she pounced on it, a number with no name attached. Back to work. "Anna Lawler," she said breathlessly. "How can I help?"

"You need to come back out here." The voice of Virgil Haynes filled her ears. "Them steers ain't getting any better. You need to dose them again."

Chapter Fourteen

The last place Anna wanted to go today was the Haynes ranch, but she went for the sake of the cattle. She couldn't let them suffer because they were owned by dangerous jerks.

She took comfort that Callie knew exactly where she was going. As a precaution, she also called Deputy Harrison and told him about the appointment.

"This way, if I don't come back, you know where to start looking," she finished, only half joking.

"You be careful," Harrison said. "But don't worry. Could be that me or Sanchez wander that direction on our patrols today."

"If I need help, trust me, I'll make it known," Anna said. "By the way, I ran into Manny Judd. He's a good kid. I wanted to tell you that out of the blue, for no apparent reason. Making conversation."

Harrison chuckled. "My sister is a good judge of character ... so far. But I appreciate you putting in a good word for him."

"I'd love to see Manny have a chance," Anna said. "He had an unfortunate start in life."

"I know he did. Tracy's a compassionate person who wants to help everyone she meets. I don't want to see her disappointed."

"I think between you, me, Callie, Ross, and the rest of this town, we can make sure he doesn't disappoint her."

Joe's amusement continued. "It sure is different living out here. Everyone knows what I had for breakfast and what color my kitchen towels are. Anyway, you be careful. Isn't there someone you can take with you?"

She thought of Janette, but Janette would be busy with billing and ordering and answering the phone while Anna was out on calls. "No one who has time to drive all the way to a ranch and watch me inject cattle. I appreciate you keeping an eye out."

"Let me know when you're done so I can call off the posse."

"Sure thing. Take care, Deputy."

"You too, Dr. Anna."

Anna felt a little better after her conversation, and again when Virgil proved to be alone when she arrived. She saw no sign of Jarrod or Blake. While she wasn't exactly comfortable with Virgil, handling one Haynes brother at a time was preferable.

"They aren't getting well," Virgil snapped at her. "What did you dose them with, tap water?"

"It was only yesterday," Anna said. *Never be intimidated by a client,* the vet she'd worked for in San Angelo had told her. *You're treating the animals, not the dickhead owners.* "Medicines take a while to work. It won't hurt if I top them up, but you have to give it a few days."

"Right, and I have to keep paying for the top-ups."

Anna tightened her jaw. "Tell you what. I'll charge you for the medication because it costs me, but not for the call out."

"You're damn right you won't charge me for the call. And you'll charge me half because I already paid for the first dose."

Virgil towered over her, face red, big fists clenched. Anna lifted her chin and looked him right in the eyes, even if she had to crank her head back to do it.

"I'd turn around and drive out, but I want your cattle to recover," she said clearly. "So you'll pay me for the dose, or you can call another vet."

"Ain't no other vet in River County."

"Then you don't have a choice." She bravely turned her back and walked to the corral where the steers watched her hopefully.

"You are some bitch, Lawler," Virgil called after her. "How about this? I'll pay you for the whole dose but you go down on me before you leave. We'll call it even."

Anna's skin crawled. She turned around when she reached the pen and the safety of the big animals. "No, Virgil. Then I'd just have to charge you more."

Virgil stared at her a long moment, then he laughed, a loud braying sound. "You have balls, woman. Fine. Whole dose. Put it on my tab."

Virgil, chuckling at his own wit, disappeared into the office and slammed the door.

Anna slid into the pen and approached the first steer. "Let's get you well so you can get back to the range and away from him," she said quietly.

She wished the cattle weren't so pathetic. The pen stank horribly from their runny manure and their misery.

These steers had ear tags, some handwritten, some printed. A few of the local ranchers had gone to electronic tags, although those were only good within a certain range, and she knew that a simple metal wall could interfere with the signal. Anna doubted Virgil would fork out for electronic tags and software for animals he was just going to take to a feed lot.

Anna finished medicating the animals and patted them, talking to them as she liked to. They responded to her voice, gazing at her with sad eyes. Jarrod and Blake never appeared, which was fine with Anna.

On any other ranch, she'd pop into the office after she washed up, letting the ranchers know she was done and on her way, and she'd email them a bill if they didn't want to pay her now. But the idea of walking into the office where Virgil lurked made her queasy. And who knew when Jarrod and Blake would appear?

Whatever. She cleaned her hands under a spigot, the water pipe warmed by the sun, and fled to her truck.

RAY INSISTED HE DRIVE KYLE TO THE CLINIC SO HE COULD have his bruises checked. Kyle went without resistance, knowing Ray would give him hell if he didn't, and to assure himself that Blake hadn't cracked his ribs again.

Kyle's doctor examined him without a word, but it was clear even he had heard about the fight and Kyle's date with Anna. Kyle loved Riverbend, but damn, it was gossipy. The doctor at least cleared him, saying he'd staved off being too badly hurt, and prescribed acetaminophen for the pain.

The best thing about the day was Anna's phone call. Kyle

tried to play it cool when he answered, but her soft voice asking if he was all right made him buoyant.

It was too soon to ask her out again, Kyle had admonished himself, and simply ended the phone call. He repeated this throughout the day whenever regret hit him.

Ray left after lunch, saying Drew really needed more help. With the drywall, he added quickly.

"Drywall," Kyle said, straight-faced, as Ray put on his hat. "Is that what you kids are calling it these days?"

"Shut the fuck up, Kyle," Ray growled and slammed out of the house.

Kyle laughed at him. Something was going on there, and once Kyle figured out his own life, he'd pry it out of Ray.

Kyle spent the evening alone. He made himself stay home, take a hot shower to soothe his aches, and watch TV. The phone sat next to his hand. He kept staring at it, thinking he should call Anna.

No, too soon.

Why too soon? Were there rules? And who made them up?

If he called her, where would he ask Anna out to? The diner? A movie? The nearest movie theater was in White Fork, and it had one screen for its six-month-old films. Everyone in town would have streamed the movie before it ever reached River County.

There was Grace's bakery, but it wasn't open in the evening. Kyle could invite Anna to the ranch for dinner, maybe have Grace cater it, though she likely wouldn't be able to spare the time. Grace had a husband and two kids, not to mention her bakery. Her own life.

Kyle could always throw something on the grill. What? Eggplant? Mushrooms? Zucchini?

Lame. If Kyle invited Anna over, she'd guess he wanted her to stay the night.

Would she say no right away? Or be happy to?

Shit, why couldn't they just go for a walk or something?

Because he was sore, and she worked all the time. Hell.

Kyle threw his phone across the room. It landed on a chair and slid harmlessly to the rug.

He gave up and went to bed. Where he lay most of the night, reliving every glorious second of being with Anna. Her taste, her skin under his fingertips, her mouth on his, the wonderful sounds she made when she came.

Any sleep was filled with dreams of her, them doing it in impossible positions in weird places. The best parts of the dreams were her smile, her beautiful eyes, and the fact that she was with *him*.

Kyle woke in the morning, hard and needy. He went to the office, not looking forward to another long, empty day.

"Where the hell is Ray?" he asked Margaret when he sat down behind the desk.

Margaret blinked at him and made a show of looking around the room. "Not here. I assumed he was having breakfast. Or already in the barn."

"Nope. I didn't hear him come home last night. Hmm, that's suddenly interesting."

Margaret shook her head. "You boys. If he married her, he'd settle down and get back to work. You too."

"We can't both marry the new owner of the B&B," Kyle tried to joke. "I think that's illegal in this state."

"You know I'm talking about Dr. Anna." Margaret frowned, her tanned face creasing. "Buy her a ring, set a date. You waste so much time dancing around things, when you could be enjoying life together. Grace did the same thing with Carter, and now look at her. Radiant."

Kyle listened in surprise. "I didn't know you were such a romantic, Margaret. Who's the guy?"

"Who *was* the guy, you mean." Margaret's expression softened, her brown eyes almost tender. "I had a wonderful marriage for twenty years, but we could have been together so much longer if we'd admitted right away that we were meant for each other and stopped fighting it. Seven years we dithered, thinking we had all the time in the world." Her softness evaporated and she slammed a clipboard to the desk. "But we didn't. Life's a bitch, and diseases don't care about your happiness. So don't waste a single second."

Kyle's distractedness fled in a wave of sympathy. "I'm so sorry. I never knew."

"That's because I don't talk about it, and I don't wallow. Bill and I had a wonderful life, and I have no regrets. But watching you and Ray flounder around these women you obviously are in love with ticks me off. Stop wasting time and quit making such a big deal about it. And don't stare at me with your mouth open. You look like a fish."

Kyle obeyed. "It's great advice, but only if the liking goes both ways. If I ask Anna and she blows me off ..." He made a motion like scattering dust. "That's it."

"Then you'll know, won't you? Instead of always wondering?" Margaret glanced out the window. "Well, that's lucky. Now's your chance."

Kyle looked up to see Anna's truck with her shoeing trailer pulling in. He stared for one moment, his heart banging painfully, before he sprinted out of the office, the door slamming in his wake.

Chapter Fifteen

A nna felt Kyle's presence behind her before she turned, planning a nonchalant greeting.

But when she saw him, every gorgeous inch of him, his hat shading his face, she couldn't stop her smile. Then she tried to suppress it. She shouldn't seem too eager. Should she?

"Hey." Kyle's word was casual, but he breathed hard, as though he'd been running. "What's new? You know, since yesterday."

Anna shrugged. "One of your horses threw a shoe. Margaret asked me to come put a new one on."

"That *is* news. No one told me." Kyle reached for the portable forge and helped her lift it from the truck and set it up on its stand. "Did you know Margaret was married before?"

"Yes." Anna let him leverage the forge in place, then she checked the propane and brought the forge to life. "They lived in Austin, and her husband was a professor at UT. He died about ten years ago."

"Shit. Where have I been?"

"Busy." Anna smiled again, in spite of her best efforts. "Margaret didn't tell me that—I heard it from a friend who knew them in Austin."

"Figures. Not that I've been paying attention. Kind of wrapped up in my own life."

"Easy to do," Anna said as she adjusted the forge's temperature. "I've been coasting along thinking Janette, my assistant, will be around whenever I need her, but she got accepted into the pre-vet program at A&M. Which is much more important than cleaning out cages and doing overnights with animals for me, but it will leave me in a tough spot when she goes."

"Bet a few of the high school kids in Riverbend would be happy for a part-time job," Kyle said.

"Yes, and I'd be grateful, but I need someone older and more permanent as well. The kids can't check on animals at two in the morning."

"True. I'll ask around."

"Thanks."

While they talked, Kyle helped Anna lay out her tools and shoe blanks. She pointed out where things should go, and he positioned them with expertise.

He went to meet one of the stable hands who led out the horse, and then Kyle took over securing the horse while Anna went over its hoof with her rasp and began to fit the shoe.

They worked together so seamlessly that a warmth began in her heart. Too bad they couldn't have a conversation that wasn't stilted and awkward. Strangers on a bus spoke with more animation than Anna and Kyle.

"What have you been up to?" she asked as she worked. "Besides getting into fights at the feed store?"

"Oh, nothing much. Catching up on paperwork at the office. Healing. Exciting times."

They'd gone out twice and had great sex, and now had nothing to say to each other. This sucked.

"I went out to the Haynes ranch again yesterday," Anna said as she waited for the shoe to heat in the forge. "Virgil, the jerk, wants his steers to magically heal overnight. I'm thankful his brothers weren't there and that Virgil was too busy to harass me much."

She heard a profound silence. Anna tugged out the shoe with her tongs, tapped it on the anvil, doused it in water, and looked up to see Kyle with a face like thunder.

"What?" she asked. "I injected the cattle and left. Quick as I could."

"I'm serious, Anna. Don't go out to that ranch again. Not alone. Take Janette at the very least."

Anna carried the shoe back to the horse. "Life isn't that simple. One, it's my job to look after sick animals. Two, it's not the cattle's fault their owners are jerks. Three, I told you, Janette's leaving soon, and I need her at the clinic instead of babysitting me on my calls."

Kyle's scowl deepened. "The Haynes boys are dangerous and they wouldn't hesitate to hurt you if they wanted. They think they're unstoppable."

"I know." Anna needed to narrow the shoe a tad. She stuck it in the tongs again and thrust it back into the forge. "I went for the cattle's sake."

"You're not obligated to take their calls. No one is forcing you to be their vet."

Anna watched the shoe until its ends were red hot, then

she dragged it out and set it on the forge. "I have a small window of time to tap this into shape, and arguing about the Hayneses isn't helping."

"I'm saying it's smarter not to deal with them," Kyle said in a hard voice. "Not because they picked a fight with me— we've been scrapping since we were kids. But Blake could have killed Sherrie and her horse and doesn't give a shit. Only reason Virgil worries about Blake being found out is because she'd make a claim on his insurance—if they even have any—and if Blake gets himself thrown in jail, he can't help out at the ranch. Thinking of you out there with them, by yourself ... It makes me crazy."

Anna banged on the shoe and then plunged it into the bucket of water, enjoying the satisfying hiss of steam. She rose with the shoe clutched in her tongs.

Kyle stood with his arms folded, his hat shading his scowling face. He was delectable, green eyes sparkling and animated.

Anna relented. "I'd tell you that you were an overbearing, overprotective shit, and that I can't base my life on what will and won't make you crazy ... but I think you're right. I talked to a vet I know in Llano County, trying to get him to take over the Hayneses as clients, but he refuses to deal with them."

"Smart guy."

Anna grinned as she took the cooled shoe to the horse and laid it against his hoof. Perfect. "We talked about luring an unsuspecting vet to River County, just for the Haynes brothers, but we couldn't figure out who we could trick. We like the people we knew in vet school too much to do that to them."

She hoped Kyle would laugh, but he remained stony.

Anna fitted the shoe and tapped one nail in. She reached for the next, and found it handed to her by strong, tanned fingers. Anna murmured a thanks and continued affixing the shoe.

They finished in silence, Kyle handing her nails and leading the horse back to its pen while she stripped off her work gloves and washed her hands under the nearest spigot, applying the hand sanitizer she kept in her pocket. Kyle returned to help her put away her things, the two working quickly and efficiently.

Anna's forge needed to cool down before she could load it, which meant she'd have to hang out for a few minutes. She usually spent the time answering phone calls and checking appointments, but Kyle put his hand in hers and led her to the house.

Once inside, Kyle hung up his hat and scrubbed off his hands in the sink. Anna started to say, "Are we going to argue some more?" but Kyle swiftly dried off and came to her.

Her words died as he gazed down into her eyes. Kyle cupped her face in his hands and drew her to him, taking her mouth in an abrupt and then lengthening kiss.

KYLE COULDN'T GET ENOUGH OF HER. ANNA WAS HOT AND perspiring from her work, her body pliant beneath his hands, her mouth a place of heat. Her hands landed on his chest, and she parted her lips to kiss him back with enthusiasm.

Not a lady who took well to being pushed around. Anna pushed back.

But Kyle didn't want her near men like the Haynes brothers. He wanted to wrap himself around her and protect her, to keep her from bullies and assholes all the days of her life.

Anna's kiss was as strong as his, she rising on tiptoes to reach him. She clung to him, pushed at him, her body crushing into his and sending fire through his blood.

Kyle ran his hands down her back as the kiss eased to its end. "Wow. I should get you mad at me more often."

Her voice was shaky, her eyes shining. "That's not hard. Mostly you just have to talk."

Kyle laughed softly. Somehow he'd ended up with his back to the kitchen counter, Anna against him. Not a bad place to be.

"Wanna stay for lunch?" he asked. "Or does lunch piss you off too?"

"I have appointments." Anna looked up at him in consternation. "I think."

"Just a snack then. Let's see, what do we have?" Kyle reached for the refrigerator door a foot away and swung it open. His hand landed on a bottle in the door tray, and he pulled it out, closing the refrigerator and cutting off its pleasant chill. "There's this. I used to suck it straight from the container when I was a kid. My mom would yell at me something awful."

He turned around the black plastic squeeze bottle. Chocolate syrup, made for squirting onto a big bowl of ice cream.

The flare in Anna's eyes made him instantly hard.

"We start like this." Kyle popped the top of the bottle and dribbled out a line of chocolate on his finger, which he licked clean. Anna watched in fascination.

He lifted Anna's hand and trickled some onto her finger,

and before she could lick it herself, he caught her finger and sucked it into his mouth.

"Mm," he said.

More heat in her eyes. Kyle smeared chocolate on her lips and leaned down to kiss it off.

The kiss was sweet with the dark bite of chocolate. Kyle got lost in sliding his tongue into Anna's mouth, the two of them licking chocolate and kissing.

The next thing he knew, Anna had twisted the bottle out of his hand. "Better take off your shirt," she advised.

Kyle had his T-shirt stripped from his body before the kitchen clock could tick once. A second later, cold chocolate landed on his belly, tingling and tickling. Kyle laughed.

His laughter died when Anna bent down and licked the chocolate from his skin.

"Baby, you ..." Kyle's words tangled as Anna's tongue found his navel. "Shit."

He sucked in a breath as Anna tugged his belt loose and then opened his jeans, the zipper hissing in the quiet.

"You aren't really going to do that." Kyle had no idea why the words came out, because hell yes, he wanted her to.

His cock tumbled out as Anna yanked down his jeans and underwear. He was stiff with wanting, dark with need. Kyle yelped as the chocolate landed on his cock, the syrup chilled from the refrigerator.

He balled his fists as Anna sank to her knees and took him in her mouth.

Son of a bitch. The heat of her tongue and the brush of her teeth slammed heat through him until he wanted to yell. His heart beat thick and hard, his need to thrust building into fever pitch.

"Damn." The word was a growl. "Anna, what the fuck are you doing to me?"

He shouldn't have said anything, because she backed away, removing the incredible sensation of her mouth. Her face as she gazed up at him with cornflower blue eyes was the most beautiful thing he'd ever seen.

"I don't know," she said, cheeks pink. "Seemed like it would be fun."

Kyle snatched the bottle out of her hand and blobbed chocolate on his cock, putting up with the cold. "It is. It is fun."

Anna laughed. She swiped her tongue over the chocolate, her smile gorgeous.

Kyle wanted her naked. Naked and covered with chocolate.

Right now, she had her tongue all over him, her lips smooth as she kissed, licked, sucked him.

"Shit," he repeated softly.

He slammed the bottle to the counter and raised Anna to her feet. They couldn't do this here. Someone would come in —Ray, Margaret, Grace—whoever. They'd find Anna and Kyle tangled on the table in a pool of chocolate. His family would either be shocked, delighted, or take pictures and text them to their friends.

Kyle dragged up his jeans and grabbed the bottle. "Come upstairs," he said rapidly, and led the way out.

Chapter Sixteen

❧

As they went up the stairs, Kyle kept looking behind him as though he feared Anna would race back down, jump into her truck, and charge off.

She could. Anna knew she had no more appointments today, in spite of her earlier memory blank, but she should get back to the office in case someone came in or called with an emergency.

Then again, any emergency calls would be forwarded to her cell phone in her pocket. Therefore, Anna could follow Kyle to his bedroom right now and jump his bones if she wanted.

Kyle's room wasn't what she expected. It was a suite, for one thing, taking up most of the top floor. One room held his trophies and belts, photos of himself bull riding or receiving his prizes, and newspaper and magazine articles clipped and framed.

Anna saw this as she rushed by and into the room under sloping eaves that held a bed and a dresser and not much else.

"Nice view." Two dormer windows, one on either side of the bedroom, looked out over the rolling hills toward the river. Anna had seen Kyle leaning out of the front one the day he'd watched her at her forge.

"Moved up here when Ray and I took over the ranch. Ray kept his old room, but I kind of got over the whole bunkbeds thing."

Anna laughed, the sound shriller than she liked. Kyle's current bed was wide with a thick bedspread, neatly made. She wondered whether Kyle was fastidious or the cleaning crew took care of it.

As Kyle stood awkwardly, hanging onto his loose jeans, Anna grabbed the bottle of chocolate from him and thunked it to the dresser. "Need to hurry. I'm on call."

Kyle immediately sat down and yanked off his boots, throwing them aside, jeans following. "I don't want to be the only one getting naked here. Come on. Let's see some skin."

Anna shivered with agreeable heat. She turned her back, unable to make herself unbutton her shirt in front of him, but she popped the buttons without hesitation, wanting this playfulness.

Kyle came to her and helped her slide the shirt off, leaving her in her bra. He turned her around, took up the bottle, and squirted chocolate all over the top of her breasts.

His grin made his eyes sparkle. "Mm, sundae."

Anna gasped as he leaned down and licked her, his mouth hot, his warm, wiry hair brushing her chin. She kissed the top of his head.

Kyle's hand went to her back, and he unhooked the bra. "Don't want this getting messed up." His voice was soft, coaxing.

"No, we don't," Anna murmured.

More chocolate, this time running between her breasts and encircling her nipples. Anna went incandescent as Kyle wove his tongue around each nipple, suckling them clean, taking his time.

She undid her jeans herself, pushing them down to bare the swirl of hair that was growing moist. Kyle slid his fingers between her thighs and found her heat, their eyes meeting as Anna dragged in a breath.

He moved his fingers, watching her, bringing her to life. Anna rocked on his hand, the residual chocolate on her breasts smearing his chest.

Fire roared through her as she arched against his touch, her cries building as Kyle's fingers danced. He enveloped her, his larger body enclosing her smaller one, curving over her as though shielding her from the world.

Anna clutched him frantically, her hips moving. She wanted nothing more than to drag him inside her, feel his hard body on hers, keep this white-hot sensation going on and on.

Kyle feasted on the chocolate on her breasts as his fingers continued their magic. He was smiling hard when he raised his head. His beautiful touch went away, but he caught Anna in his arms and carried her to bed.

He used his own stash of condoms this time and soon was sliding into her, increasing the madness inside her.

Anna held him as he thrust, loving his firm weight, the strong warmth of his body. She rose to meet him, the feeling of him inside her transporting her to a wild place she'd never been.

Like last time, Kyle wasn't quiet. He groaned, said *damn* a dozen times, and then everything became incoherent but her name. That was loud and ringing, the sound sweet and honest.

Anna came as Kyle thrust harder, faster, her frenzy building with his. She cried out wordlessly, sounds echoing in the large room under the sky. Sunshine poured through the west window, warming them as they rocked together, light touching Kyle's body of liquid bronze.

Kyle's final thrust made Anna shout. He went perfectly silent, holding her with his eyes, jade green and dark with desire.

"Kyle, I lov—" Anna began, before Kyle's kiss silenced her.

Just as well. She'd done enough foolish things for one week.

KYLE LED ANNA BACK DOWNSTAIRS AN HOUR LATER, THE TWO of them giggling like little kids. Anna's hair, which she'd tried to stuff back into a braid, was a mess, chocolate staining her cheeks. Kyle had it all over his neck and chest, and a glance in a mirror showed him a smear across his jaw.

He'd fetched the bottle of chocolate off the dresser after they'd finished making love the first time ... which had led to the second time.

Kyle halted abruptly when they entered the kitchen, and Anna bumped into him. Then she saw what had startled him, and turned very red.

Ray turned around from the refrigerator, a bottle of water in his hand.

Kyle's heart beat in hard jerks. "Ray. What are you doing here?"

"I live here." Ray moved his slow gaze to Anna. "I take it you're done upstairs? Good, because I want to have lunch."

Anna's face was brick-colored, which clashed with the chocolate on her cheek. "Don't worry, I'm outta here," she said rapidly. "Have an office to get back to."

"Better swing home and wash up," was Ray's advice. "So no one thinks you were mud wrestling."

Kyle growled. "Fuck you, Ray."

Ray looked surprised. "I'm not trying to be an asshole. Just save her some embarrassment."

"No, he's right," Anna said. "Everyone's already talking enough. See you, Kyle."

She charged out the door. No good-byes.

Ray motioned after her with his water bottle. "Better walk her out, or she might never come back."

He had a point. Kyle snarled again at his brother and raced after Anna.

"Hey." He reached her as she loaded her forge, and helped her lift it into its trailer. "Sorry about that."

"Not your fault. We weren't in a good position to hear him come in."

Kyle's anger dissolved in a flash. "I don't know—I thought it was a pretty good position."

He expected her to give him a look of scorn, and then dive into the truck and take off, but Anna flushed, her eyes starry.

"So do I."

They laughed, everything funny for some reason.

Kyle cupped her cheek, his amusement dying. "A while back, you started to say the L word." He shook his head. "I'm not worth it, Anna. I'm just a dumb fuck who falls off bulls."

When Anna looked up at him, he spied in her eyes something he'd never seen from any other woman.

"You are worth it," she said softly. "And whenever you do let someone say the *L* word to you, you'll deserve it."

Kyle's mouth went dry. He should say *he* was the one in love, that he'd never met anyone like her. That when Anna walked into a room, he saw no one else. But his lips wouldn't move, and his tongue stuck to the roof of his mouth.

Anna's phone buzzed, making him jump. She heaved a resigned sigh and slid her phone from her pocket. "That's Janette texting me. I have to go."

Kyle knew that. Anna was busy, sought after, needed.

She closed the trailer and climbed into the pickup. Kyle shut the door for her as Anna started up. She gave him a faint smile through the open window and eased the truck forward.

"Anna!"

She halted, looking back at him in polite inquiry.

"Um." Damn it, why was it so hard to ask a simple question? "Want to go out again?" he said in a rush. "This Saturday night?"

Anna's answering smile untwisted something inside him. "Well, yeah. Better not be someplace that serves chocolate," she continued, unaware that his heart was turning over and his brain was mush. "We can't be trusted around it."

Kyle burst out laughing, and she joined in. Her beautiful smile flashed as she pulled out, dust rising in her wake as she left the ranch for the road to town.

KYLE WENT BACK TO THE KITCHEN AFTER ANNA HAD GONE TO

find Ray building himself a mountainous sandwich from various things in the fridge.

"You home to work?" Kyle asked him. He leaned against the counter and folded his arms. "Or are you rushing back to the B&B?"

"Told Drew I'd do more for her this afternoon." Ray put away all the condiments then carried the finished sandwich to the table, sat down, and took a large bite.

"What are you now, her contractor?" Kyle asked.

Ray chewed and swallowed, his frown deepening. "The place is a wreck, and Drew has to make a go of it in a year, or she loses it *and* all the money he left. So says her grandfather's stupid will. He wanted the family back in Riverbend so much he stipulated that if she can't turn the B&B around, she loses everything. The whole inheritance."

Kyle felt a dart of sympathy as well as irritation at Old Man Paresky. "That sucks. Can't she contest it?"

"She's been to see lawyers about that. No, she can't, and she's decided she doesn't want to. She's taken with Riverbend, wants Erica to go to school here."

"Huh." Kyle helped himself to a bottle of water and joined Ray at the table. "You really like this woman, don't you?"

Ray had lifted the sandwich for another bite, but he set it down, slowly wiping his mouth. "Yeah, I think I do."

"You sure?" Kyle unscrewed the water and took a long drink. His throat was parched from all the yelling upstairs, but it had been worth it. "You haven't gone out much since Christina dumped you, and then the whole thing with you maybe being the father of her baby."

"Which I wasn't," Ray pointed out with a narrow look.

"I know. But it kicked your ass. You didn't say much, but I could tell."

"That was two years ago, Kyle. I've moved on."

But Ray hadn't moved on until a little while ago. He'd thrown himself into work and bull riding and had ignored the women who blatantly chased him. Kyle wasn't certain his brother'd had sex since Christina, which was unhealthy, in Kyle's opinion.

"Have you?" Kyle asked.

Ray made an exasperated noise. "You know, this is why I don't bare my soul to you. You jab at me like a mother hen. I have moved on, yes, and yes, I like Drew. I think maybe—you know—I'd like it to be permanent."

"Holy shit." Kyle sat up. "As in marry her? I've never even met this woman."

"Not my criteria for asking a woman to marry me—*Have you met my little brother?*"

"You know what I mean. What if she's a con-artist taking you for all you're worth? You know, your dry-walling skills and everything."

"She's not." Ray's voice went hard. "If you want to meet her—fine, you can meet her. But do me a favor. Wait until I've asked her. Then if she says no, I'm spared having to bare my soul to you again. I can let it go."

From the look in his eyes, Kyle knew this one Ray *wouldn't* be able to let go. He'd invested, and Ray didn't invest in people lightly.

"What about you and Anna?" Ray asked abruptly.

Kyle hid a start. "What about us? I thought we were talking about *your* problems."

"Now she's a *problem*, is she? Seemed like you two were pretty friendly. At least from all the noise coming from the third floor."

"Anna Lawler is the sexiest woman alive," Kyle said

without hesitation. "We're having some fun. I think that's all."

"You *think* that's all?"

"Yeah." Kyle thought of Anna's impulsive. *Kyle, I lov—*

He'd cut her off before she could say the whole thing. If she regretted the words later, came to him and told him she didn't mean it, Kyle didn't think he'd be able to stand it. It would tear out his heart, and he wasn't ready for that kind of pain.

Ray laid his hands flat on the table. "I'm going to tell you something. The entire town—no, the entire county—knows you and Anna are getting hot and heavy. They all like Anna. In fact, they *love* her. If you toss her aside, they will jump on you so hard there won't be much left of you. What Blake tried to do to you yesterday will be nothing. Anna has that many people on her side."

Kyle made a noise of exasperation. "Why am I suddenly the bad guy? I go out a couple times with Anna, and now everyone thinks I'm going to dump her? She's the one who will do the dumping, and we all know it."

"Mm, I don't think so. Not with the way I saw her looking at you. Tell you what. You ask her to marry you, and when she says *no*, you're off the hook. You tried, but you let her do the dumping." Ray opened his hands then returned to his sandwich. "They'll have to give you that."

"You mean, I look like a total idiot and let her kick me with her sexy cowboy boots, and they won't come after me with sledgehammers?"

"You got it. Now get back to the office and let me finish my lunch in peace."

Kyle climbed to his feet. "You're all heart, Ray."

"Oh, and if you're wondering who took the rental car and turned it in for you yesterday morning, it was me."

Kyle stopped halfway across the kitchen and swung back. "You? Why?"

"To save Anna embarrassment," Ray said. "So her neighbors wouldn't see your car still there in the morning. Everyone knows you were there anyway, but the car was proof."

Kyle took in a slow breath while he thought it over. Ray was right, but at the same time ...

"So it was better that I ran through the alley in my suit and got beat up at the feed store?" he asked.

Ray nodded. "Took the pressure off Anna."

He said this without guilt. Kyle longed to throw something at him, but nothing was handy. He also wanted to laugh and agree with him.

"You're all heart, Ray," he repeated and went out, slamming the back door.

His irritation at his brother evaporated as he walked back to the office. The ideas Ray put forth in the stupid conversation stayed with him.

By the time he returned to his desk, Margaret giving him a severe look, a plan had formed. The plan might leave Kyle looking like the biggest idiot in Riverbend's history, but as Ray said, this wasn't about Kyle.

Chapter Seventeen

Kyle, I love you.

As she drove from the Malory ranch, Anna hid a groan. How stupid was she? Of course Kyle had stopped her from finishing the sentence—did the gentlemanly thing and said he wasn't worth her affection. Anything to get her to shut up.

She had to wonder how many women had said it to him. He must be tired of hearing the phrase by now. How embarrassing.

And yet.

Anna knew she hadn't exaggerated. She hadn't been caught up in the moment. There was a reason she couldn't stop thinking about Kyle's broad smile, his amazing eyes, and the drawl that made her whole body tingle.

There had been a reason she'd dressed up as a rodeo clown and been in the ring when Kyle had taken his fall. Not, as she'd told Callie when she'd first had the idea, to see what really went on behind the scenes at rodeos. Not entirely.

She'd done it to make sure she could help Kyle when he needed it.

There had also been a reason she'd raced to his ranch nearly every day after that, on the flimsiest of excuses. And a reason she hadn't curled her lip and walked away when he'd asked her to dance at Ross and Callie's wedding.

Anna had wanted Kyle's arms around her, his body swaying against hers as they danced. To hear his laughter, see his eyes upon her.

She had to face it—Anna was totally and madly in love with Kyle Malory. Had been for a while.

Back at the office, she tried to answer Janette's questions about the billing that she'd texted about, but Anna could only stare at the computer as the numbers danced and made no sense.

Janette was excited about starting classes at A&M in the spring, and they took a break from the billing to talk about that.

"You'll be forever labeled an Aggie," Anna warned jokingly. "Despised in Longhorn country." The rivalry between UT Austin and Texas A&M was legendary.

"Worth it." Janette gave her a grin. "Who says I'll even be working in Texas afterward? I might go to California. Or North Carolina. Or somewhere I've never been."

The possibilities were endless at age twenty-one. "If you do large animal, you'll end up in a small town in the middle of nowhere," Anna said. "That's where most large animals live."

"Racehorses don't," Janette said dreamily. "I could work on beautiful horses and save their lives and a grateful billionaire would marry me." She twirled and laughed at her fantasy. "But I'll more likely live in the middle of Nebraska and make sure the cows give good milk."

"A person can find happiness anywhere." Anna tried to look older and wiser. "Even here in Riverbend."

"Like you with Kyle?" Janette gave Anna a sly grin. "He is hot, Anna. I can't fault your taste."

"And this conversation needs to end." Anna's phone rang, and she lifted it gratefully. "Saved by the buzz. Hello, this is Dr. Anna."

Kyle? Janette asked silently.

Anna shook her head as she listened to a rancher called Kennedy asking Anna in his slow way if she'd mind stopping by if she had time and looking at some of his steers that were down with diarrhea.

"No problem at all," Anna said brightly. "I'll be right there."

Anna logged the call into their computer system, grabbed her bag, and headed out.

Janette raised her brows. "You'd rather race off to a bunch of shitting cattle than talk about Kyle?"

"Yep." Anna bent her a severe look. "You'll have to make that choice when you set up practice."

"Let's see. Hot guy, cows with the runs." Janette tapped her cheek. "Oh well, those are the breaks. Go on. I've got the office."

Janette waved her off, and Anna went, torn between mirth and mortification.

The Kennedy ranch wasn't far out of town. When she pulled in, the place appeared deserted, but she knew there'd be people around somewhere. She headed to the corrals behind the barn and found a few ranch hands with what looked like the steers in question.

Hal Jenkins, who'd shown her the ropes as a rodeo clown, was one of the hands. He greeted her then got down to business in his characteristic reserved fashion.

"I'll load one into a chute for you," he said. "Poor guy's in a bad way."

A young steer went into the chute, bawling in terror. Anna soothed it, patting its shoulder while she took a sample of blood and then scraped up some of the feces readily flowing out of his backside. Rubber gloves were her friends.

Scours again. Not uncommon, but not good if it was widespread.

"If it's a parasite or infection, it's contagious, and these guys should be isolated for a while," Anna said. The symptoms in these steers were very like the ones in the Hayneses' cattle, which worried her. "Where were these guys pastured? Have they come into contact with anyone else's cattle lately?"

"Don't think so," Hal said. "But I do know some cattle have gone missing from here."

Anna gave him a sharp look. "Missing?"

"Sure. Happens sometimes, especially when they're young. We figured coyotes got them."

The men around Hal nodded.

"How many, exactly?" Anna asked. "Can you tell me tag numbers? Brands?"

Hal's eyes narrowed. "Sure. Mr. Kennedy keeps good records. Why?"

"I'm not sure yet. Might be nothing."

Hal frowned but gave her a nod and strode heavily toward the office.

Anna medicated the steer and the others that the men patiently led into the chute for her. Hal returned after a time with a list that he shoved at Anna as she stripped off her soiled gloves.

"If you can find them, Kennedy would be grateful," Hal said. "And then you might explain why you won't tell me where you think they are."

"Because I don't know yet if I'm right. I promise, though, that if I find Mr. Kennedy's steers, he'll be the first to know. You'll be second."

Hal scowled at her. "You're lucky I like you, Anna. And trust you."

"Thanks, Hal," Anna said sincerely. "That means a lot."

Hal helped her pack up and walked her to her truck. So different from working with the Haynes brothers, where she hauled her own stuff and fled as soon as she could.

Hal lifted her heavy medical bag into the truck and looked in as she got into the driver's seat.

"Tell Kyle that if he dicks with you, I'll kick his ass."

Anna gave him a weak grin. "I'll be sure to give him the message."

"The Malory boys are trouble. Their sisters are the only ones worth anything."

"I have to agree with you about Kyle's sisters," Anna said as she started the truck. "Grace and Lucy are sweethearts."

"And seriously good looking." Hal's face softened. *Interesting.* "But Grace got herself hitched to Carter Sullivan of all people, and Lucy ran off to work with billionaires in Houston." He shook his head, lamenting the loss.

"Grace is deeply in love and very happy. Lucy, from what I hear, is having fun being a corporate executive."

Hal rolled his eyes. "She's a small-town girl at heart. She just don't know it."

"I am too," Anna said. "But I had to figure that out for

myself. And who knows? Maybe Lucy will take to big-city life just fine. A lot of people do—hence, why so many live in big cities."

Hal gave her a tolerant smile, as though he knew better about Lucy. He slammed the door and patted the top of the truck, his way of saying good-bye.

Anna put aside the intriguing possibility of Hal's feelings for Lucy and pushed the button on her steering column to dial her cell phone.

"Hi, Kyle," she said when he picked up. "I need to head to the Haynes ranch. Can you meet me there?"

KYLE FOUND ANNA INSIDE HER PICKUP, WHICH SHE'D PULLED to the side of the road not far from the gate to the Haynes ranch. He slowed his truck to halt behind hers.

The road remained empty, this stretch always quiet. Kyle figured he could set up a picnic lunch in the middle of it and be polishing off the food before another vehicle came by.

He hopped out of his pickup and sauntered to Anna's, leaning on her open window while she gazed ahead of her, lost in thought.

"Hey, lady," Kyle drawled. "Can I check under your hood?"

"So funny." Anna turned to him, her beautiful eyes troubled. "I think the Hayneses are stealing cattle."

Kyle's brows shot up. "Rustling?"

While people might laugh and think cattle rustling had disappeared with the Wild West, they'd be wrong. It still happened, except with semi-trailers in the middle of the night instead of bandits on horseback—although there still could be some of that. A herd of cattle was worth a lot of money.

Anna nodded. "I was just at the Kennedy ranch. Hal Jenkins told me they're missing cattle, and their steers have the same problem as the ones I treated for the Hayneses. Hal didn't notice the scours until now, but the cows have been out on the range a while, so who knows how long they've had it? I thought I'd better check things out."

"Damn." Kyle pushed back his hat and wiped his forehead. "Any proof?"

"I don't know. Hal gave me the tag numbers of the missing steers. Plus they have the Kennedy brand, though brands can be altered."

Kyle acknowledged this. Crossbars or symbols could be added over the original brand or an N changed into an M, or something. The alteration wouldn't stand up to extreme scrutiny, but most people didn't look closely without cause.

"I wish I could say I'm surprised." Kyle adjusted his hat against the breeze that was growing stronger. "But you don't have to confront the Hayneses if you don't want to. I found another vet to take over their calls."

Anna blinked, startled out of the immediate problem. "What are you talking about? What vet?"

"A friend of Margaret's." Kyle folded his arms on the open window. "He lives in Lampasas but doesn't mind coming out here to help. He's a big guy, like an ox, but loves animals and won't take shit from anyone. Margaret called him."

"Oh." Relief warred with determination in her eyes, and relief won. "That was nice of you. I might take you up on that. *After* I find out if they're cattle rustlers."

"Did you call Ross?" Kyle asked.

"Not yet. I'd rather have at least some proof before I do,

so I won't be just a paranoid vet complaining about bad clients."

"Commendable." Kyle took off his hat completely, leaned in, and gave her a quick kiss. "And thank you for calling me to come with you."

Anna flushed, her lips parted from the kiss. "I'm sometimes overly confident and maybe rash, but not stupid. I'm not setting foot on their property without backup."

"Aw. I'm backup. That's so sweet."

"Shut up," Anna said softly. She looked at him as though she wanted to kiss him again, maybe stay out here and keep on kissing, but she squared her shoulders. "Come on. Let's get this over with."

Kyle locked his truck and joined Anna in hers. She drove across the cattle guard that marked the boundary of the Haynes ranch, and down the dusty drive toward the corral and office.

Blake's shiny pickup was parked near the office but Kyle saw no one around. Anna turned off her truck and gazed ahead of her in dismay.

"Where are the steers?" she asked in bewilderment.

The corral she stared at was empty. Anna slid out, turning in a circle to take in the stables, corrals, and trailer that held the office. No animals could be seen except two horses who dozed in mare pens in the shade. Kyle expected the horses to yawn any minute.

Anna took off for the office. Kyle leapt after her, jogging past her to reach the trailer before she could.

"What were you saying about being rash and overly confident?" he asked in a quiet voice.

Anna glared but made a show of stepping back and

letting him go in first. Kyle knocked on the trailer door and pushed it open before invited.

Virgil was there all right. A rodeo groupie with her shirt off knelt in front of him, Virgil's cock in her mouth. She jerked back when she heard Kyle come in, and Virgil flinched. She must have bitten him in her haste.

The young woman shot to her feet in alarm, arm over her bare breasts, then she recognized Kyle and relaxed.

"Hey, Kyle." She gave him a big smile. "Want to join us?"

Kyle growled at Virgil. "You couldn't lock the door?"

Virgil scowled, eyes glittering in fury. He snatched at his jeans, trying to pull them up, but he couldn't before Anna pushed around Kyle and caught him with his butt exposed.

"Where are the steers?" Anna demanded.

Virgil took his time settling his underwear and zipping up his jeans. Anna kept her eyes on his face, as though she hadn't noticed him half naked and couldn't care less. But then, she saw a lot of penises in her job, if not human ones.

"What steers?" Virgil asked her, pretending ignorance.

"The ones I was treating for scours," Anna said angrily. "I told you to keep them isolated or your entire herd might get sick."

"Oh, they're isolated. I just moved them."

"Where?"

"None of your damned business."

Anna balled her fists. "How am I supposed to treat them if I don't know where they are?"

Virgil slowly buckled his belt. The young woman had sidled to Virgil's desk and lifted a T-shirt from it, turning her back to put it on. Kyle stepped in front of the door so she couldn't run off.

"I thought you were done treating them," Virgil said to

Anna. "And mad at me for calling you a second time. And now here you are, out of the blue. With Malory. What the fuck is going on?" He blasted the last question at Kyle.

Before Kyle could answer, Anna said smoothly, "I need to give them a booster or they could get worse. It's only a dozen steers, but that's money down the drain if they don't get better."

Kyle watched the wheels turn in Virgil's head. He didn't trust Anna's glib words but he hated the thought of losing money. Cattle he couldn't sell were useless to him.

"Fine," Virgil said, his jaw tight. "They're in a pen at the end of the farm road. Take a left at the dead end and go down a dirt track about half a mile. I'm holing them up there until I can turn them out."

"Good." Anna gave him a satisfied nod. "I'll give them a last dose, and they should be fine."

Virgil didn't answer her. He folded his arms as he contemplated Kyle. "So why are *you* here, Malory? Or is she fucking you in her truck between jobs?"

Anna rolled her eyes and marched out without another word.

Kyle grinned at Virgil. "I should be so lucky. And to quote you, that's none of your damned business." He turned to the buckle bunny who hovered uncertainly. "Tina, how you doing? You need a ride back to town?"

Tina glanced at Virgil for guidance, but he remained stonily silent. Kyle hadn't noted any vehicle but the Hayneses' on the property, so she likely was relying on Virgil for transportation. She might come to regret that.

As Virgil clamped his lips together and didn't answer, Tina said to Kyle, "Sure, if you're heading that way."

Virgil finally glared at her. "If you leave with Malory, sweetheart, don't ever come back."

Tina again wavered, but Kyle sent Virgil a pitying look. "Like that's going to keep her awake at night. You ready, Tina?"

Tina made her decision and nodded. She caught up a purse she'd left on the desk and hurried out, not saying good-bye to Virgil. Virgil watched them go, a silent hulk.

Kyle wasn't sure what Anna would say when he ushered Tina out, but she didn't comment at all as Kyle opened the back door of Anna's pickup and helped Tina inside.

"Thanks for the ride, Dr. Anna," Tina gushed as she settled in. "But you don't have to. Virgil said he'd take me, or I can hitch."

Anna turned to her in astonishment. "No way am I letting you hitchhike. It's too hot, and it's dangerous." She started the truck, and as soon as Kyle had buckled himself into the passenger seat, she pulled away. "But I have to find the steers first."

"No problem." Kyle gestured to the road they were approaching. "Tina can take my truck back to town."

Anna flashed him a puzzled glance, but after they grated over the cattle guard she slowed next to Kyle's truck. Kyle handed Tina a fob with a single key.

"Drive it to the diner and give the key to Mrs. Ward. I'll pick it up later. You'll be okay from there?"

"Sure." Tina beamed Kyle a huge smile as she took the fob. "Thanks, Kyle. You really are the best."

"That's what they tell me. And hey, Tina." Kyle spoke through the window as Tina jumped out and slammed the back door. "You can do way better than Virgil. Don't trust him. There are plenty of other cowboys at the rodeo."

Tina seemed to at least listen to him. "Yeah, you're probably right. See you, Kyle. Dr. Anna."

She flashed them another smile then jogged across the road to Kyle's truck. Anna waited until Tina started up, did a U-turn, and drove away.

"You just gave her the key to your truck," Anna said. "And you think *I'm* reckless."

Kyle shrugged. "Everyone in the county knows that's my pickup, so if they see her taking off with it, they'll report it. Besides, Tina's a good kid, just ... misguided. Thinks chasing men is the way to have fun and be taken care of. She'll park it at the diner, like I asked her to."

When Kyle finished, he found himself the object of Anna's shining gaze.

"What?" he asked, growing nervous.

"She's right, you are the best. You have a great heart, Kyle Malory."

The heart in question swelled with something almost like pain as Anna stepped on the gas and shot them down the farm road, heading into sunshine.

Chapter Eighteen

❧

T he steers were exactly where Virgil had said they'd be. Anna pulled over outside a large corral made of wooden fencing in the middle of a vacant lot.

"No shade and a makeshift tank of water," she said in disgust as she slammed her truck's door. "Asshole."

The steers looked up listlessly as Anna and Kyle approached. They appeared to be physically better, which meant Anna's medication was working. But they looked listless and sad, as neglected animals do. Anna wondered if Virgil was even bothering to have someone feed them.

They perked up when they saw Anna and began to wander toward her. Anna climbed the fence and waited for the first steer to approach her. "Here we go. Is this one on the list?"

Kyle perched himself on the fence above her and consulted the clipboard he'd carried from her truck. The small steer's ear tag read 386.

"Yep. I have a 386 here," Kyle said. "He have Kennedy's brand?"

Anna ran her hand down the steer's back until he turned so she could see his haunch. Though tagging and chipping were common now, ranchers still branded their cattle with their ranch's logo. Freeze branding had mostly taken over hot branding as both easier to read over time and less painful for the cattle.

Kennedy's brand was an upside down U with a crossbar. This steer had an upside down U with an X through it.

Ranchers used similar brands, but what were the odds that Kennedy and Virgil had ones that close together?

"Hang on." Anna rubbed at the patch of hair, which had grown in white. "This part of the X is paint. Stupid."

She scrubbed at it, while the steer watched her calmly. Half the X came away, leaving Kennedy's brand clear to see.

Kyle whistled. "Man, Virgil has some balls. Check another, in case this one is just a stray."

Anna patted the steer and walked to another. That one had been painted too, and was another of Kennedy's, but the next had a different brand and a number not on the sheet.

"Legit?" Anna wondered. "Or stolen from someone else?" She looked around the pen. "Wait a minute." She caught another steer by the horn and rubbed at his haunch. "Isn't *your* ranch's brand a lazy M?"

She pointed to the letter M on the steer's side, which had been painted into a simple square. "Are you missing a number 238?"

"I don't know," Kyle said. "Ray's been managing all the cattle, and he hasn't said anything. But yeah, that looks like one of ours."

"Hard to notice if one or two disappear," Anna said charitably. "Like Hal told me, you figure coyotes or a stray found by someone else."

"Ray hasn't been paying attention, so don't be too nice to him. But Virgil is an idiot. If Ray finds out Virgil rustled his cattle, Ray will rip his balls off."

"Well, this one was stolen from you," Anna said. "Let me check a few more."

Several of the steers were on Kennedy's list, and a couple had other brands, all painted over. Anna finished and leaned against the fence where Kyle sat, his blue-jeaned legs at her eye level.

"I wonder if any of these steers belong to the Hayneses at all," she reflected.

"I'm willing to bet he stole his whole damned herd." Kyle thumped the clipboard. "Fucker. We need to call Ross now."

"Yep." Anna laid her hand on his thigh, liking its hardness under worn denim. "I'd say we have some evidence."

———

KYLE HOPED THAT WOULD BE THE END OF THE HAYNES brothers—plus he had an idea about how to prove Blake had caused Sherrie's accident.

But Ross couldn't get a warrant until the next day, and when he and his deputies went to arrest Virgil and family for cattle theft, they found the Haynes boys at home, looking innocent, and no sign of any cattle. Every single steer, including the dozen Virgil had penned, were gone.

Kyle had come along to show Ross where Virgil had stashed the steers, but the gate was open, the tank drained and scummy. Only the imprints of hooves showed any cattle had ever been there.

"Guess you had a wasted journey, Interim Sheriff," Virgil said to Ross when he and Kyle confronted the brothers in their office. Virgil gave Ross a grin. "There haven't been steers at this ranch for a while. I don't know what Dr. Anna told you, but she's a little loopy." He circled his finger near his temple. "She might be dipping into her tranquilizers, or just wants to get into Kyle's pants. The Malorys and us have a rivalry going way back. You know, like they do with the Campbells. They'll say anything to make us look bad."

Kyle knew damn well Virgil was lying, but as Anna had said, Ross couldn't do anything without evidence.

"Yeah, I want to get him too," Ross said to Kyle as they walked away, Sanchez and Harrison heading in disappointment toward their SUV. All three Hayneses watched from the doorstep, looking smug. "Those cattle had to have gone somewhere. They didn't have time to take them far. I'll try to find out if he paid someone to haul them away, and where."

"Or, he just drove them onto the open range." Kyle scanned the green hills, as though he'd see steers popping up to turn themselves in. "But I came up with another way to at least help prove Blake caused Sherrie Bates's accident the other night." Kyle nodded at Blake's gleaming pickup. "He's got a dash cam. Saw it when I was here yesterday."

Ross's eyes lit. "Nice. Now let's hope it was on and he didn't destroy the feed. I'll need to get another warrant to look at it, but …" He grinned at Kyle. "I don't think I'll have any trouble with that. Thanks, Kyle."

"You're welcome. I'll keep a lookout for those steers, though. Convicting the Hayneses for cattle thieving will get them out of our lives faster than reckless driving."

"True. Though Blake can go down hard for a hit and run." Ross looked cheerful. "Oh, by the way, Callie's doing a big fundraiser in a couple weeks, for her rehab ranch. We're having a huge cookout, bands, the works, at the Jones house.

She'd love it if you and Anna came. Oh, wait, Anna probably already told you."

Kyle stared at Ross, his face slowly heating. Anna hadn't mentioned it. "You mean come as a couple?"

Ross frowned. "Aren't you a couple?"

"I don't know." Kyle stood still, a wave of unhappiness flowing over him. "I really don't know."

Ross gave him a comforting pat on the shoulder. "Well, Callie thinks you are, and she's pretty smart. I'm sure you'll figure it out."

"Great." Kyle followed Ross, who moved with a spring in his step toward his SUV with *River County Sheriff's Dept.* on its side. "I'm glad someone knows for sure. 'Cause it isn't me."

Ross sent him a sympathetic look and leapt into his SUV, eager to round up a judge and another warrant.

Kyle gave the Haynes ranch a final glance—all three brothers lingered to watch them leave, smart-ass grins on their faces—and drove slowly back to town in his own truck.

True to her word, Tina had left his pickup at the diner yesterday, the key with Mrs. Ward. Mrs. Ward had given Kyle an admonishing look when he came in for the key, saying Kyle didn't need to be chasing Tina while he was going out with Anna. Mrs. Ward hadn't relented until Kyle explained Anna had been with him at the time, and he'd given Tina the truck so he could keep helping Anna.

Like Ross and Callie, Mrs. Ward now assumed he and Anna were a couple. And wanted them to stay a couple.

Ray was right that the whole town would crucify Kyle if they thought him using Anna for a quick bounce before he chased after rodeo groupies again. He needed to put his plans in motion fast, before they formed a lynch mob.

Kyle reached home and called Anna as he parked. Her phone went to voice mail, which meant she was working. Kyle told her briefly what had happened with the Haynes boys and promised they'd talk later. He hung up and went inside the house.

There he found his sister Lucy.

She lay face down on the sofa in the living room, wisps of her dark hair, which had grown out from its severely short cut, straggling across her cheek. She was in jeans and a T-shirt instead of her usual smart suit, and she was crying.

All out, heart-wrenching bawling.

"Lu?" Kyle tugged open the curtains of the dark room, letting in a flood of sunlight. "What are you doing here?"

Lucy raised a tear-streaked face, glaring at him with red-rimmed eyes. Lucy and Grace looked a lot alike, but where Grace was softness and curves, Lucy had the angles of a runway model. Although right now she looked like his gawky little sister crying because mean kids kicked her.

She rubbed at her wet eyes. "What do you mean, what am I doing here? This is still my home, right? Or did you clear out my room?"

Kyle gentled his voice. "I meant, why aren't you in Houston in your sleek condo? The one with automatic everything." The last time he'd visited, she'd proudly showed off her voice controls to open and close the curtains, answer the door, start the coffeemaker ... Everything but pee for her.

Lucy's face crumpled. "Because I got *fired!*" The word dragged into a sob.

"What?" Kyle pulled a chair to the sofa and plunked himself on it. "*Who* fired you? Your hot billionaire boss? I thought you and he got horizontal on a regular basis."

"We did. But now he's getting *married.*" Again the last

word broke. "He had a big party and said he was making an important announcement. Then he brings out this beautiful woman and gushes all over her, saying she said *yes*." Lucy trailed off bitterly. "Of course she did. She's the daughter of his dad's old business partner and she'll bring a ton of money and investors to his business. The next day, he cleared out all his loose ends, which included *me*."

"Aw, sweetie." Kyle gathered his sister into his arms, his heart burning as she collapsed onto his shoulder.

He guessed what must have happened—Lucy, being Lucy, would have confronted the guy about this sudden decision to marry, and bossman, realizing Lucy wouldn't put up with being kept on the side, dumped her. Then fired her, to make sure she wasn't in his office day after day. He'd want Lucy as far away from his new wife as he could shove her.

"I'm so sorry, Lu." Kyle rumpled Lucy's hair as he'd done when she'd been young and vulnerable—which she still was, he realized. "Want me and Ray to go kick his ass?"

"No," Lucy mumbled. She raised her head and gave him a feeble smile. "I mean, yes, I'd love it, but it wouldn't make any difference. I don't have a job, or a career. The man I thought loved me doesn't give a shit about anything but staying in the Fortune 500. So now I'm old and unemployed, single, and a total loser."

"No you're not." Kyle held her again, rubbing her back. "You're not old by any stretch of the imagination, and you'll never be a loser. You just trusted the wrong guy. Can happen to anyone. Look at Ray now—he wasn't paying attention, and the Haynes brothers stole our cattle. Some of them anyway."

As he'd hoped, Lucy's tears let up in a flicker of curiosity. "Seriously? They always were shitheads. Where is Ray? I went down to the office, but Margaret says he hasn't been around for a while. She looked very irritated about it."

Kyle let out a chuckle. "That's because Ray's got a girl-friend. Or at least we think so."

Lucy looked even more curious, so Kyle filled her in on everything that had gone down since she'd last called. At the very least, Lucy looked interested in Ray's awkwardness and less sorry for herself.

"I need to meet this woman." Lucy turned a knowing gaze on Kyle. "And you with Dr. Anna. Way to go, bro."

Kyle raised his hands. "I don't know if I'm *with* her or not. Not yet, anyway. Tell you what—wash your face and we'll go to the diner. Food here sucks without Grace to cook it."

Lucy's eyes widened in panic. "No, I can't. Everyone will want to know what happened, why I'm here. I can't go through that."

"Not if you spin it right." Kyle put a soothing hand on her arm. "Tell them you got tired of big city life and wanted to come home. They'll believe that. Have you talked to anyone else?"

"Just Margaret, but I didn't tell her the whole story. I'm sure she knows there's more going on than I'm saying, but she didn't ask." Lucy looked limply at Kyle. "But it's true. I did want to come home. When everything fell apart, all I could think of was running here. Where I'd be safe."

"And welcome." Kyle hugged her again. "And loved, little sis. Now, let's go get us some dinner. I'm starving."

Anna sat in her office, staring at a map of River County on her laptop screen. Satellite photos gave her an eagle-eye view of the world, though she thought it a little creepy too. Anyone could zoom in on her office or her street and house and see a lot of detail. The photos were static and months old, but still ... The give and take of technology.

Right now Anna roved River County via map to figure out where Virgil might have stashed the stolen cattle.

Virgil, who wasn't quite as stupid as everyone supposed, must have caught on that she and Kyle figured out he'd rustled the cattle. Between the time they'd left and Ross had been able to get a search warrant and show up, Virgil and his brothers had gotten rid of the evidence.

But Anna could see no way they'd had time to round up *all* their cattle, most of which had been roaming their vast acreage, load them into trucks, and take them off to a feed lot or slaughterhouse or even to another ranch. Not alone, and not without anyone noticing. So the cattle couldn't have gone far.

Anna wished she could type in "Find cattle Virgil stole in or near River County" and have the computer zoom in on them, but no.

The trouble was, there were many places he could have driven them. The river created folds in the land, long hills, steep drops into box canyons, and plenty of caves. Evidence of ancient peoples had been found all over the Hill Country, and even now a team of archaeologists were working north of Riverbend on a site from what they called the archaic era. A few cattle wandering around would seem like part of the scenery.

Anna sighed and shut her laptop.

Janette had already gone for the day, and no animals were there for an overnight. The office was silent, eerily so.

Anna rarely found the quiet oppressive. She'd always

been an introvert, liking peaceful places out of the hubbub of life where she could read or think.

But today, the empty office seemed lonely. She shut everything down and went home to feed Patches, who was always happy to hear food clinking into his bowl. Anna fixed pasta for herself, slurping up the noodles drowning in tomato sauce with mushrooms.

A tap on the front door startled her. She answered it to find a beaming Mrs. Kaye on the porch.

"Kyle was at the diner," she said. "I just saw him. Then he headed to the bar." She leaned closer, conspiratorially, but she had a twinkle in her eyes. "With another woman."

A knot tightened in Anna's stomach, and she found it suddenly hard to breathe. "He's allowed," she managed to say. "We're not a couple. Or exclusive. Or ..." Her throat tightened, and she had to cough. *I'm just in love with him. Doesn't obligate him to me.*

Mrs. Kaye bathed her in a sudden grin. "Oh, honey, I didn't mean to upset you. I'm only teasing. He's with another woman, that is true—but it's his sister Lucy. She came home. Probably for good. Isn't that nice?" She shook her head. "It's about time that girl figured out that all she needs is right here in Riverbend. Just like Grace did. And you. That's why *you* came back, isn't it?"

Anna stared at Mrs. Kaye, her head spinning with relief. Kyle was with his sister. Not another woman, like the feather-headed Tina.

She realized Mrs. Kaye waited for her to answer the question. *Why* had Anna returned to Riverbend? Because she wanted her own practice, or because she knew this was where her heart was? Or both those things?

"I think so," she ventured.

"Of course you did. Now, you don't want to stand here and talk to a dithering old biddy like me. You get yourself to the bar and say hi to Lucy and be with young people."

Anna sent her a faint smile. "I've been with people plenty today. Quiet night with the cat for me. I need it."

Mrs. Kaye studied her a moment, then her benevolent expression vanished. "Anna, honey, if you ask anyone around Riverbend who knew me back in the day, they'll tell you I was a wild girl. And they'd be right. I was all about drinking and dancing and showing off my legs—I couldn't settle down for nothing. And then I met Mr. Kaye. I took my sweet time figuring out I was in love with him and the whole marriage and family thing was for me. But once I did—we had decades together, grew closer and closer each passing year. You can have that with Kyle—I see it in his eyes. But you can't have it if you shut yourself in your house watching life pass you by. Go out and live it. Be with your friends. Most of mine are gone now. Enjoy the hell out of them while they're alive. Trust me on this."

Anna listened, her lips parting. She'd never seen Mrs. Kaye so adamant.

Having delivered her sermon, Mrs. Kaye's smile returned. "Listen to me run on. You go out, Anna. Find Kyle, and have a good night."

Without waiting for Anna's response, Mrs. Kaye turned and hobbled down the porch steps and back to her house, humming to herself.

Anna retreated inside and stood in the middle of her living room, reflecting on what Mrs. Kaye had said. *Hidden depths*, was the term.

Patches watched sleepily from his cushion, then raised a paw and daintily licked it.

Anna let out a long sigh. "Screw it," she said, and left the house.

She walked the short distance to the heart of Riverbend, the night cool and comfortable. The diner's lights glowed with welcome, as did those of the bar beyond it. Many Riverbenders ate dinner at Mrs. Ward's then rounded out the evening with drinks, pool, and hanging with friends at Sam's tavern.

Anna rarely went to the bar—she was either too exhausted after work or didn't have anyone to meet. She'd gone with Callie from time to time, but now that Callie was married, their girls' nights had become fewer and farther between.

Hal Jenkins lounged on the porch in front of the bar with a few of his friends, including Jack Hillman, and some of Jack's biker buds.

Hal sprang up and opened the door for her. "Evening, Dr. Anna."

"Hey." Anna gave the guys a shy smile and a nod. She had no idea what to say to them when she didn't see them in the context of work.

Hal and friends didn't seem to mind, just went back to talking after she slid past them and into the bar.

The interior was dark, but not so dark no one could see each other. Anna quickly spotted Ray at the bar nursing a beer and gazing indulgently at his sister Lucy, who was halfway across the room at Kyle's side. She and Kyle laughed and talked with townsfolk who seemed excited to see her.

Lucy's smile was too brittle, her gestures too animated. Something had happened, something not good. Anna remembered Lucy's eagerness to shake the dust of Riverbend from her feet and knew she wouldn't have come home on a whim.

She lingered on the outskirts of the conversation, hearing Lucy saying things like, "Oh, I needed a break from the never-ending traffic." Or, "There's really no place to get a better steak than Mrs. Ward's. I'd dream of her food."

Kyle stood shoulder-to-shoulder with Lucy, and Ray looked on protectively. Kyle fielded questions that were tough, such as, *Weren't you dating that rich guy you were working for?*

Anna understood the gist. Whatever relationship Lucy'd had with her billionaire boss was over, and she'd retreated to Riverbend to lick her wounds.

Kyle hadn't noticed Anna in the shadows yet, Anna holding a beer she'd barely sipped. He was solidly with his sister, shielding her from too much prying, too much heartache.

Anna's heart warmed. He was that kind of guy.

"Um, Dr. Anna?"

Anna turned at the sugary voice and found herself face-to-face with Tina.

Tina bathed Anna in a perfect smile. She topped Anna by six inches and had a chest that thoroughly filled out her T-shirt. But in spite of the smile, Tina looked troubled.

"What's up?" Anna asked, hoping she didn't have to give buckle-bunny relationship counseling. And she did *not* want to think about whether this young woman and Kyle had ever—

"Virgil dumped me," Tina broke her thoughts by saying. Anna braced herself to explain, in detail, why Tina was better off, but Tina continued, "And that's fine, because he can be kind of an asshole, but I won't get my calf."

Anna blinked. "I'm sorry. Your what?"

"My baby calf. He's so adorable, and Virgil promised I could have him. But now he won't call me back, and I heard all his cows are gone. Do you think you can talk to him? He listens to you."

Virgil didn't listen to anyone, but that wasn't the point. "When did he tell you could have the calf?"

"When I was helping him feed it. It needed a bottle and it was *so* cute. He was going to kill it—it wasn't calving season and it would be too much trouble, he said—but I talked him out of it, or thought I did. It came in with some others he got, but I guess it couldn't find its mother."

"Tina." Anna faced her, holding her gaze. "This is important. Where did Virgil feed this calf? And were there other cattle there with it?"

"Sure. There's a sort of big field between steep hills. He has a feeding area there, where cows could come in and get hay at night if there wasn't enough on the range. He kept the calf there, but it's hard to get to, and Virgil won't answer the phone. I'm so worried." Her eyes filled with tears. "I don't want him to kill it."

Anna caught Tina's hands, squeezing them in excitement. "Tina, I'll take you there. Can you tell me exactly where it is?"

"I think so. Thank you, Dr. Anna," Tina gushed. "You're so nice."

"Hang on, just a sec." Anna hurried to Kyle's side, giving a quick nod to Lucy's startled, "Oh, Anna. Hi."

Anna clutched Kyle's sleeve. "Can you come with me? And we should call Ross, and ... everybody. And bring Ray along. And Hal and Jack—they're outside. I think I might know where to find the stolen cattle."

Chapter Nineteen

The long twilight stretched overhead as Kyle drove down the ranch roads Tina pointed out.

Anna sat next to him, Tina in the back, the young woman leaning forward to give directions. Tina couldn't remember exactly so they'd backtracked a couple of times, but after she'd peered around in silence for a few turns, she gave a little hop on the seat.

"This is right. I remember now."

Kyle had been down the lanes off this road before, but not for years, and the last time had been on horseback. They might need horses if Virgil hid the cattle too far down this canyon.

The river that ran through it, Welk's Creek, was an offshoot of the Colorado, and was alternately dry or flowing, depending on the rains. Welk's Canyon curved through land that could look flat, but was full of sudden drops, washed out gullies, and arroyos that could hide all manner of things. Kyle had done climbing here before, with Ray, though it had been a while.

The sun had firmly set by the time Kyle reached the end of the ranch road. A makeshift gate ran across where it petered out, the area to either side fenced off by two rows of barbed wire between evenly spaced wooden posts.

Several vehicles pulled up with him. Ray was behind the wheel of one, with Hal as his passenger. Behind them came Carter Sullivan and Tyler Campbell, followed by Ross and Harrison in a sheriff department's SUV. Deputy Sanchez brought up the rear, pulling a horse trailer with four horses ready to go.

All was quiet. A few rabbits scampered away from the lights, and in the distance coyotes yipped. Wind stirred the grasses on the side of the road, but Kyle saw no sign of cattle.

"It's farther on," Tina said. "We had to hike to get to it."

Kyle and Anna had already discussed the idea that Tina might be leading them into an ambush with the Haynes brothers, but they'd dismissed it. First, Tina had always been honest and forthright, and Kyle doubted Virgil would trust her to do any luring. Second, he and Anna hadn't come alone, in the gathering darkness, without backup or anyone knowing where they were.

"I'll take a look," Kyle said. When Tina started to open the door, Kyle held up a hand. "You stay put. You too." He pointed at Anna. "If I find anything, I'll let you know."

Anna nodded, not happy with sitting still, but she also wasn't about to run headlong into danger. Let the sheriff with his gun go ahead of them.

"Don't hurt the calf," Tina pleaded.

"I won't," Kyle promised her.

Tina was just a kid, he reminded himself, barely into her twenties. He hoped for her sake that Virgil hadn't simply brought the animals out here and slaughtered them all.

Ray met him at the gate, which Kyle unlatched. Ray said nothing, but his face was grim. Hal joined them, and Ross led the way, shotgun held ready.

Kyle and Ray shared a look, then they walked forward together.

"DAMN, COWBOYS ARE HOT," TINA OBSERVED AS THEY WATCHED the guys in jeans and cowboy boots walk past them. "So are deputies," she added as Joe Harrison strode by in his crisp uniform. "Joe is the cutest ever, isn't he? Think he'd go out with a white girl?"

Harrison wasn't all that much older than Tina in years, but he had smarts and far more life experience. "Maybe," Anna said diplomatically.

"Kyle is super-hot too. I drooled over him for a long time. Oh. Sorry." Tina shot Anna a guilt-stricken look. "I forgot. You're into him. Well, don't worry, Kyle never went out with me, not in the sex way. Treats me like a little sister or something. Says I'm too young for him. I don't think I am, but whatever. I'm glad now we never did it, because it would be so cool for you and Kyle to be together."

Something inside Anna untwisted. She hadn't wanted to come out and ask Kyle if he'd ever had Tina in his bed, but deep down she'd wanted to know.

But she should have realized there'd been nothing going on. Kyle was a guy who liked women, yes, but he wasn't a total man-whore, grabbing any female who walked by.

"I was going to wait a few years and try again with him," Tina said. "Though I don't know. Once I'm old enough, in his opinion, he'll be something like *thirty-five*." Anna heard the implied *Ewww.* "But anyway, he's with you now." She ended on a happy note, glad everything had worked out.

So everyone said.

Kyle came out of the dark to stand by Anna's door. Anna didn't see him at first and jumped, letting out a yelp.

"Easy there," Kyle said through the window. "Come on. We need your expertise."

Anna's pulse, which had finally calmed, sped again. She hoped Kyle hadn't returned to lead her to sick, wounded, or dying animals. She knew the reality of putting down animals to ease them from pain and fear, but she hated doing it— hated the necessity of it.

Kyle didn't look morose or angry, which gave her hope. She fell into step behind him as they moved from the road to a narrow and dusty path, which grew darker as they went. Kyle flicked on a flashlight, the beam slicing through the night.

Tina trotted behind them, uninvited, but Anna didn't have the heart tell her to go back to the truck. Anna wouldn't have been comfortable in Tina's tiny skirt, cropped shirt, and cowboy boots that were more for show than use, but Tina seemed unbothered.

Anna followed Kyle over humps in the muddy path and around boulders, deeper into the canyon. They walked for about a mile, and Anna's respect for Tina rose as she kept up without fuss or hesitation.

Anna's feet were growing sore by the time Kyle halted them. More flashlights cast shadows up the canyon walls as Ross and the others explored.

The path ended at a fall of white rocks that climbed to a flat plain above. Makeshift feeding bins and pens had been built here, but they were empty, no cattle in sight.

"What did you want me to see?" Anna asked.

"Well." Kyle looked embarrassed. "We were hoping you could tell us what cattle had been here, how long ago, and where they went."

"Seriously?" Anna looked at the cowboys she'd known most of her life, and they looked back at her without blinking. Expecting her to know. "I'm not a tracker. I can't glance at a clump of feces and tell you they're six miles west in a pasture eating clover."

"I know, but you can tell us *something*," Kyle said.

He gazed at her in complete trust. So did the others. When she'd first started her practice here, most of the ranchers hadn't believed she could be any good. Except Kyle, she realized. He'd trusted her judgement every time she'd come to look at their animals—she just hadn't seen it.

Anna shrugged at the same time her heart warmed. "All right. Let me look around."

Kyle handed her his flashlight, which she shone around the ground. The land had been trampled, making it obvious cattle *had* been here. The feed bins contained the remains of hay, some of it still green. And she found feces all right. All over the place, much of it fresh.

"I'd say they were here earlier today," Anna said. "And went that way." She pointed and gave a faint laugh. "West."

"Can you tell if any were hurt or weak?" Kyle asked.

Anna flashed the light around. "No, this all looks like healthy poop. And I don't see any hoof prints that are odd or skewed, like the animal was hurt. Doesn't mean one or two weren't, but I think they were all driven out of here—*driven* as in let out and chased off. Is there any evidence of trucks picking them up?"

Ray shook his head. "We didn't find any, no."

Anna handed Kyle his flashlight. "Virgil hid the stolen cattle back here," she summed up. "And when he feared Kyle and I might stumble on the truth, he and his brothers drove them out onto open range, off their property."

"Letting the evidence wander away," Kyle said, scowling.

"Oh, well. We need to find the cattle, no matter whose property they're on, and return them to their owners."

Ross nodded and lifted his radio. "Come join us, Sanchez. Bring your friends."

A clatter of hooves followed his words, Sanchez leading the now-saddled horses. Ray silently mounted one, Hal following. Ross scrambled aboard another.

"Just like an old-timey sheriff," Tina said, laughing at Ross. "Aren't you going to ride, Deputy Harrison?"

Harrison shook his head, his face tight as he gazed at the tall horses. "Not really my thing."

"Well, you can do just as good on the ground." Tina sidled closer to him, her smile admiring.

Harrison looked down at her with alarm. "Um. Let me go back and call this in. We'll need more riders."

He swung around, out of Tina's reach, and escaped, striding off into the darkness alone. Anna stifled a grin.

Sanchez mounted the last horse and the riders headed out, leaving Anna, Kyle, and Tina, who shivered as she looked around. "I think I'll wait in the truck," Tina said in a small voice.

Kyle nodded at her. "That's probably best."

Anna opened her mouth to say she'd take Tina back when the silence was broken by a terrified yell. Not from one of the men, but from an animal, the long "Maaaa!" of a frightened baby.

"My calf!" Tina spun around, wildly searching the darkness. "That's my calf! I know it."

"Could be." Anna stood still and scanned the rocks. The calf went quiet, and Anna made kissing noises. "Where are you, little guy?" she crooned.

Rocks clacked one on another, and the cry sounded again. But no calf appeared. Kyle flashed his light up the side of a wall.

"Oh, great," he breathed.

Anna was already rushing to the rock wall, having seen the flash of eyes too far up. "Do you have ropes?"

"Think so. Tina—can you run back to the truck? Ropes are in the bed."

"Yes. Yes." Gravel crunched as Tina hurried away in her shining boots. "Just rescue my calf!"

"This won't be easy." Anna took a running start at the rock wall and scrambled up it a few feet, but the gravel was too slippery and she slid back down.

Kyle tugged on gloves and approached the rocks more cautiously, feeling above him for handholds. He turned to Anna, passing her his flashlight. "Can you give me a boost?"

Anna set the flashlight on the ground and cupped her hands around his boot. "You can get up there, maybe, but how will you bring the calf down?"

"One problem at a time." Kyle grunted as Anna shoved him upward. He caught a handhold and wedged one boot into the rocks. "Oh, and by the way. Will you marry me?"

Chapter Twenty

"What?" Anna's mouth went dry, and her ears rang. She couldn't have heard Kyle Malory just propose to her.

"I said, will you marry me?" Kyle struggled up another few feet, and the calf bawled pathetically. "I wanted to ask, in case I don't make it down."

"But then ... We ... I ..." Anna ran out of words. Pebbles trickled down the wall.

"You don't have to answer right now." Kyle's words grew fainter. "But think about it." He grunted. "Damn."

"What?" Anna yelled. "What damn?"

"Nothing. I'm gonna need the ropes."

"All right, I ..."

Anna went speechless again, her mouth ceasing working as Kyle inched his way up. She heard him slip, and curse, and catch himself, and her heart thumped in fear.

Tina dashed back, ropes draped over her arms. She also dragged a large metal box behind her, bump-bumping it over the rocks and dirt.

"I found this too," she panted. "I thought it might help."

Anna struggled with the lid of the box and wrenched it open to find tools—screwdrivers and wrenches, but also thick nails and metal wedges and bolts.

"Yes!" Anna grabbed the ropes Tina began uncoiling with competence. "If I wasn't in such a rush, I'd hug you."

Tina's eyes gleamed in the growing moonlight. "I've done three-ways before. Those can be fun."

Anna gaped at her a split second, then started to laugh. "You are awesome, Tina. Help me."

She began to cram wedges into the rocks. Tina gave Anna a boost, again competently, and Anna slowly climbed up toward Kyle.

He waited, having made it as far as he could by free climbing. Anna knew only rudimentary rock climbing, but Kyle confidently drove in wedges she handed him and tied the ropes to create an anchor. The slope was nowhere near as sheer as boulders Anna had practiced on in college and had plenty of nooks and crannies, but anchors and ropes would help them, especially in the dark.

Together they ascended, Tina's voice echoing from below for them to be careful but hurry.

The calf was trapped on a ledge just under the top of the canyon. It couldn't scramble upward to safety, and it couldn't go down without falling. It would never survive the steep drop.

Kyle kept climbing. After a moment, Anna saw what he would try—to go to the very top and haul the calf upward to solid ground.

Anna skimmed up after him, making sure she had a firm hold of the grips that Kyle had driven in and the anchors he'd tied.

Anna had almost reached him, when Kyle slipped. She stifled her shriek as he slid down the rock face, trying to stop himself with boots and hands, until he finally thumped to a halt a few feet above her.

"Damn," he growled. "I'm out of practice. Now I gotta do that stretch all over again."

Anna gave him a weak smile. She could tell him they should give up—she could try to shoot a tranq dart into the calf, a dose large enough to ease him into death.

But there was nothing to say she would succeed with the tranq dart, in the dark, from the base of the cliff. Plus, she'd have to drive back to her office to get the dart gun which she rarely used, and hope that it worked.

The calf's cries wouldn't let her simply abandon him. It was not Anna's way to give up on animals.

Kyle continued to climb, no slipping now, as though determination gave him a better grip. He reached the top of the wall, thirty or so feet from the ground.

"Come on." He held his hand down to Anna.

She caught it, scrambling upward to the top. Anna hauled herself over the edge, Kyle assisting, and landed on her back on prickly grass, staring up at the stars.

The stars were blotted as Kyle leaned to kiss her. The kiss was swift, fierce, hard. Before Anna could gather herself to respond, he was up, helping her to her feet.

Together they jogged across rocky ground to where the calf lay below the lip of the wall.

Kyle dropped to his belly, scooting to the edge. "This won't be easy. But I have to try."

Anna knew he would. She'd witnessed his vast compassion since this crazy relationship had started—for Sherrie and her horse tangled in the trailer; for Tina; for Lucy, having to face a nosy town when her life was falling apart; and now for a forgotten calf, trapped and terrified.

Anna had tried to despise Kyle for being a bull rider, a rodeo star, but she'd never been able to make it stick. She'd been wrong, she was pleased to admit. Kyle was like no man she'd ever met.

And he'd just asked her to marry him. She was still reeling from that.

They worked together to free the calf as though they'd been a team for years. Anna held on to Kyle's legs as he inched his way forward and leaned over the lip of the cliff to find the calf. The calf cried out in hope and began to scramble.

Anna quickly passed Kyle ropes. He had the beast tied, four legs tamed, with the quickness of a champion. Then came the tricky part of hauling the calf upward.

Anna's heart beat thick and fast, but she made herself remain calm, holding Kyle steadily as the calf thrashed and churned. She watched in cold fear, expecting Kyle to lose hold of the ropes, for the calf to fall to its death, pulling Kyle with it.

Kyle hauled the calf up, inch by inch. The calf ceased struggling after a time and went limp, as though finally understanding it was in good hands.

"It just gained forty pounds," Kyle said between his teeth. "Can you help me here?"

Anna got down on her stomach beside him, laying half on top of him, their four arms outstretched, hands holding fast to the ropes. They eased the calf upward in tiny increments, until finally, finally, its head and neck came over the lip of the cliff.

Kyle reached down and caught the calf in his arms, and

Anna caught Kyle. They rolled upward together, the calf smelling of mud, sweat, and fear. All three came to rest in a huddle, out of breath and trembling.

"Not sure this is what Tina meant by a three-way," Anna muttered.

"What?" Kyle started to laugh. "A stinky three-way." Somehow his lips found Anna's, and he kissed her in joy, relief, exhaustion. "We're good together, Anna Lawler."

"Yeah," Anna said softly. "Yeah, we are."

She lay back in his arms, cradling the calf, who had settled into her. Kyle held Anna securely, his heart pounding against her back.

"Beautiful night," he said into her ear.

The moon was high, at the three quarter mark, rendering the hills and rocks silver. The stars spread out around it, the Dippers surrounding the faint North Star, the bright roundness of planets strung in a line like pearls.

"Yes," Anna whispered back, and she turned and pressed a kiss to his lips. "Beautiful."

KYLE ENTERED THE DINER TWO NIGHTS LATER, SWEAT trickling from his temples, worried he was late.

He wasn't—he was early, because they weren't ready for him. Mrs. Ward sent him an indulgent if stern look and told him to park himself out of the way.

Kyle hadn't seen Anna since the daring rescue of the calf in Welk's Canyon. They'd taken the poor thing to Callie's rehab ranch, Anna holding it on her lap in the back of the truck all the way. Tina had sat beside her, as worried as any mother.

The calf had proved to be unhurt, only needing a little TLC. Anna had made sure it was warm and comfortable, then had a long talk with Tina, explaining the difficulty of keeping a calf—which would grow into a large bull—as a pet.

Since Tina lived in a trailer with her mother on a tiny patch of land, she conceded they had no room for it. Anna, because she was Anna, said the little guy could stay at the rehab ranch as long as Tina wanted, where it would be well taken care of. Tina could visit any time she liked.

Tina readily went along with this. Kyle knew damn well Anna was going to pay for the calf's feed, board, and vet care, and she'd do it without worry.

"Tina's good with animals," Anna said to Kyle after they'd settled the calf and dropped Tina off at home. "I'll suggest to Callie that she volunteers at the ranch. It will give her something to do, teach her skills, and keep her away from guys like Virgil. You're right, she is a nice young woman."

And you are an angel, Kyle thought but didn't say.

He'd driven her home and given her a long kiss on her porch, but she'd been dropping with exhaustion. As much as Kyle craved her, he saw her inside then went home and let her sleep.

Ray, Ross, and the others had found the cattle. The cattle had made it easy for them, because after roaming around all day on other ranchers' lands, they headed back to the canyon. They'd been fed and sheltered there, and saw no reason why they wouldn't be fed there again.

The cowboys had spent all night figuring out whose steers were whose. Not one had actually belonged to the Hayneses. They'd stolen them all. Ross and his deputies had gone to arrest them.

Ray told Kyle that Virgil and Blake had vanished from

their ranch, leaving poor Jarrod holding the bag. Jarrod, understandably pissed off, had ratted them out in exchange for a more lenient sentence.

When state troopers picked up Blake and Virgil trying to cross the border into Mexico, they impounded Blake's pickup, and Ross was able to get the dash cam and its feed. He happily added reckless endangerment and fleeing the scene of an accident to the long list of Blake's charges.

That was the end of the Hayneses. Kyle figured Virgil would lawyer them up, but Ross was fairly confident they'd plead for reduced sentences.

Mrs. Ward and her daughters were fixing up the end of the diner the way Kyle had asked, but Kyle twitched as he waited. He tried to help a couple times, but was driven off and told to stay out of the way.

Kyle went outside into the gathering darkness and paced.

Three people crossed the parking lot to him, two adults and a child. The tall man was Ray, body bulking out his button-down shirt, hat pulled to his eyes.

Next to him was the dark-haired young woman Kyle had seen Ray with in the diner, and her daughter.

"Kyle." Ray nodded at him. "What you doing out here? Food's in there." He pointed at the diner's lighted windows.

The little girl laughed in delight. "Good one, Ray."

Ray, his crabby, bossy, older brother, looked goofily pleased.

"This is Drew," Ray said without waiting for Kyle's answer.

Kyle stuck out his hand. "Great to finally meet you, Drew. I've heard absolutely nothing about you—at least, not from my own brother."

Drew gave Kyle a sparkling smile as she clasped his hand

in a surprisingly firm grip. "Ray can be a little quiet." Drew put her hand on the girl's shoulder. "This is Erica."

Kyle took Erica's hand and winced at her enthusiastic shake. "How do you do, Erica? I'm Kyle Malory, Ray's much nicer younger brother."

"That's not what *he* says," Erica said with pre-teen frankness as she released him. "But I think Ray's pretty nice. You know, for an old guy."

Kyle grinned at Ray. "I like her." He turned back to Drew. "I hope I can get to know you better. You know, like actually talk to you, have a better conversation than Ray's cryptic grunts when I ask him a question."

Drew gave him a teasing look. "I know what you mean, because he does the same thing whenever I ask about you. The B&B is non-functioning at the moment, but we could have a cookout sometime. With—" She craned her head to look around, but no one else was in the parking lot. "Whoever you want to bring."

"Dr. Anna," Erica said. "It's Dr. Anna, right? That's who you're meeting tonight, I bet. You're all dressed up."

Kyle wore a new suit he'd gone to Austin to buy, along with his best boots and hat. He felt awkward hanging around the diner parking lot like this, but it was for a good cause.

"I *hope* I'm meeting her," Kyle said. "We'll see if she shows up."

He kept the words light, but his heart started thumping all wrong again. When he'd called Anna, casually asking her to join him for a meal at the diner, she'd said she was busy at the rehab ranch but she'd try to make it.

Kyle knew she truly was busy and it wasn't an excuse. Callie and Anna had realized that with the Haynes being busted, the Morgan ranch was empty and the absent Morgans were happy to be rid of their renters.

Perfect, Anna had said, for a permanent home for the rehab ranch. Large property, corrals, a decent office and barn ... They'd scrub the taint of the Haynes brothers from the place and move in soon.

"She'll come," Erica said with confidence. "Faith Sullivan says Dr. Anna's madly in love with you. So don't worry."

"*Erica.*" Drew gave the girl an admonishing-mother look. "That's none of your business."

Erica sent Kyle a conspiratorial grin. "Everyone knows. I love this town, even though I thought I'd hate it. There's a ton of stuff going on you'd never think in a nowhere place like this. Plus, it's really pretty."

"Erica," Drew repeated. "Sorry, Kyle. I did *not* teach her to be so rude."

Erica looked amazed. "Why is that rude? I said it was pretty."

"We're going inside." Drew put her hand on Erica's back. "Erica is quiet when she's eating."

Erica held up a hand to high-five Kyle. "Nice meeting you, Kyle. And Dr. Anna will show up. I promise." She winked and then let her mother hustle her away. Erica's voice floated back. "If there's apple pie tonight, I want a big slice. With *massive* whipped cream."

Ray, without a word, began to follow the two ladies.

"Ray," Kyle called. When Ray turned, Kyle gave him two thumbs-up. "It's a good thing, bro."

Ray studied him a moment, then nodded slowly, Ray's way of saying all was right in his world.

Ray disappeared into the diner, and Mrs. Ward emerged,

Ray holding the door for her. "Kyle!" she called. "We're ready for you."

No lowering her voice, no subtlety. Kyle squared his shoulders and walked to the door, aware that every single person in the diner glanced up at him as he entered.

Oh, well. He moved to the corner Mrs. Ward had prepared for him and looked restlessly out the window. Now to wait.

The regulator clock on the wall ticked relentlessly, mocking him.

Chapter Twenty-One

Anna hurried to the diner fifteen minutes late for her date with Kyle. She'd have to apologize but she thought Kyle would understand—helping Callie take over renting the Morgan ranch was eating a lot of time.

The ranch's owners lived in San Antonio; talking to them and waiting for call-backs was frustrating. Callie had to set up a lot of meetings, and people wanted to talk to Anna too, as the vet who would be responsible for the animals' health.

A lot to do, but this would work. Callie's dream was coming true.

The calf, whom they'd named Buddy, since he liked people so much, was recovering from his ordeal. Anna had examined him thoroughly to make sure he hadn't been hurt or malnourished. He'd been a bit dehydrated from being stuck up on the rock—how the hell he'd gotten up there in the first place, Anna didn't know, but calves could be resourceful. She hoped one of the Haynes brothers hadn't tried to hide him there, or she'd have to kill them.

She'd finally finished with a conference call between her,

Callie, and the bank that was handling the lease, raced back to town, and washed up quickly at home. Since Kyle had suggested the diner, always casual, she changed into clean jeans and a decent top, quickly re-braided and re-coiled her hair, and ran down the street, not bothering to drive the short distance.

She assumed this wasn't a real date. She and Kyle hadn't spoken much since they'd rescued Buddy, both of them busy. No conversations about where their relationship was going, or plans to go out to a fancy restaurant again, and definitely no mention of Kyle's impromptu proposal.

Which was fine with Anna. She preferred simply hanging out with Kyle and talking—much less stress. Tonight would be about two friends catching up after work. She'd ask him to go with her to Callie's fundraiser, which would be nice and safe for them, full of people.

Anna's opinion about this being a date changed as soon as she hurried inside Mrs. Ward's diner. She halted in stunned dismay, aware of every face turning to her.

The whole town must be there. Campbells filled one corner, as though they were having a reunion. Callie was with them, though Anna had hung up with her maybe twenty minutes ago. Ross must have raced her into town, sirens blaring.

Faith waved to Anna from between Grace and Carter, her smile wide. Lucy Malory sat next to Grace, looking more rested than Anna had seen her in a while. Karen Marvin shared a table with Deke, who seemed a bit confused as to why no one was paying attention to him.

Ray and Drew occupied a booth with Erica, who waved once and then watched with avid blue eyes.

The diner's inhabitants regarded Anna with interest,

gauging her reaction to what waited in the square alcove across the room.

That space had been cleared of all tables but one. A white cloth draped the table, which was laden with snowy napkins, crystal goblets, and delicate china. A bottle of wine rested in a wine bucket beside it.

A vase of roses decorated the tabletop, and rose petals lay scattered on the cloth itself as well as the lace-draped chairs. Lit candles flickered in silver candlesticks, the overhead lights turned down so the candles cast a soft glow.

Kyle stood waiting for her. He was breathtaking in a dark gray suit, a blue silk tie knotted at his neck. He'd hung up his cowboy hat, candlelight touching his glossy dark hair.

Anna's mouth went dry. She was suddenly aware of her straggling hair, her old jeans and shirt, no jewelry decorating her ears or fingers.

She was plain Anna, the shy vet, while Kyle the champion bull rider, waited in all his handsome glory.

"Oh." Anna walked forward under all those gazes to Kyle. No one spoke, the diner amazingly silent. "I feel like I should run home and change."

Kyle met her, what was in his eyes making her forget about the crush of people behind her. He took her hands, fingers warm and strong.

"You look beautiful." Kyle brushed a lock of hair from her face. "You always do."

Anna swallowed. "What is all this about? You already took me to Chez Orleans. You're off the hook for the fancy dinner."

Her throat closed up when Kyle, still holding her hand, went down on one knee.

"Anna Lawler," he said, gazing up at her with love in his

deep green eyes. "Will you marry me?" His mouth softened with a half-grin. "I asked you before, but we were a little busy at the time."

Anna gaped, heart-banging confusion coming at her as it had two nights ago. She remembered the dust and breeze in the night, the terrified wails of the calf, her adrenaline high as the two of them scaled the canyon wall.

Kyle had thrown the question at her, offhand, as someone might say jokingly when helping out in a difficult situation.

He hadn't mentioned it since, not when they carried the calf down the hill to the waiting truck and Tina, not at the rehab ranch, not in the days between. When he'd called her to ask her to the diner, Anna had assumed …

She wasn't certain anymore. About anything.

Not exactly true. Anna was very, very certain about one thing. She loved Kyle Malory, she had for a long time, and that was never going to stop.

"Kyle …" The word stuck in her throat, her breath not working.

Kyle waited, trepidation in his eyes. She understood in a flash that he hadn't set this up with the beautiful table in front of the whole town to coerce her into saying yes. He'd done it to show them he really meant it. That if she said *no*, he'd take it in stride and acknowledge it.

He was putting his heart out there for everyone to see, including Anna. He'd go with whatever decision she gave him.

Which she'd already made.

"Yes …" Anna barely heard the word, so she tried again. She put every ounce of strength in her voice so her answer would be heard in the farthest corner. "Yes, Kyle Malory, I will marry you!"

The diner erupted into cheering. Music blared, barely heard over the applause and whooping. Drew's daughter stood up in the booth, and Faith jumped to her feet and punched the air.

"Yes!" both girls yelled.

Kyle rose smoothly to his feet, still clasping Anna's hands. "I have a ring and all," he whispered into her ear. "But we'll save it for later."

Anna nodded, tears in her eyes. "You are such a shit. You should have told me it was a special occasion."

"I said, you're beautiful no matter what. I meant that." He bent closer, shutting out the laughing, celebrating mob around them. "I love you, Anna."

"I love you, Kyle." Anna let him drag her close, burying her face in his shoulder. "Damn it, I love you so much."

Kyle cupped her face and turned it up to his. The cheering grew louder as Kyle kissed her, a sweet, fiery kiss full of passion and promise.

Anna kissed him back with as much passion, and just as much promise.

She'd found her happiness, in a way so unexpected, but so profoundly *right*.

The noise wound around them, people glad to be happy with them, making their world just a little bit nicer. The Campbell brothers and their wives were being especially rowdy in the corner. Callie yelled, "I love you, Anna!"

The wave of love and friendship cushioned them, but in their private corner, Anna and Kyle were alone in each other. The kiss eased to a close, and Kyle rested his forehead on Anna's.

"I love you," he whispered.

The moment was theirs, and theirs alone.

"I love you back," Anna said. "My hot cowboy."

"Aw, you're just saying that." Kyle gave her a wide grin. "Wanna eat? It's vegetarian all the way. Not a piece of meat in sight. Not even for me. I kind of liked that mushroom thing at Chez Orleans, so I had Mrs. Ward make some."

Anna laughed. She took Kyle's hand, kissed him again, and led him to the table while Riverbend continued to rejoice.

Kyle poured wine, and he and Anna clicked glasses, toasting to their first dinner as an engaged couple, the first of many nights in the rest of their lives.

Epilogue

The fundraiser for Callie's rehab ranch took place two weeks after Kyle's proposal at the Jones family mansion on their enormous sweep of land. Cars, trucks, and SUVs filled the roped-off parking lot, and the green field behind the big white house was covered with picnic tables and lawn chairs.

Ray and Kyle helped Ross and the other Campbells stoking the grills with mesquite and getting them fired up. Grace had brought an entire restaurant with her, or so it looked from the many coolers and crates she unloaded with the help of Lucy and Faith.

Anna arrived and slid out of her pickup, jogging to assist Grace. Kyle's attention fixed instantly on her, everything in him glad.

"Hey." Ray poked him with an elbow. "You gonna light something with that or just admire the flame?"

Kyle realized he held a long-nosed lighter straight up, having clicked it on. The flame danced in the breeze and then blew out.

"Sorry. Distracted. In a good way."

Last night, he'd slept at Anna's, burrowed next to her in the bed, her silken hair on his shoulder. Even Patches landing full-weight on his ankles as they finished lovemaking hadn't upset him.

"I'm happy it worked out for you two," Ray said. "I don't know if I've told you that."

"No, because I haven't seen you. You've been at Drew's, painting and sanding and hammering, and whatever else."

"Drew needs a lot of help," Ray said. "I'm worried she won't make it. We're working hard and hired a crew, but it will be months before she can even think about opening."

"I take it you haven't asked her the big question yet."

Ray looked glum. "I don't know. She had a bad marriage, and I think she's hoping to keep out of serious relationships for a while. What we have right now is good, and I don't want to push her."

"Mm-hmm. Give her time, but don't let her slip away, is my advice."

Ray gave him a keen-eyed stare. "Now that you're engaged, you can fix everyone else's problems? You, who couldn't talk to Dr. Anna without growling at her?"

"Because I wanted her bad but couldn't admit it. I gave in and …" Kyle spread his arms. "Heaven's a great place, Ray."

"As long as you keep the noise down while you're there. Your bedroom's above mine."

Kyle shrugged, pretending not to grow warm with embarrassment. He and Anna could be enthusiastic.

"Move in with Drew, and you won't have to worry. Anna and I can run our ranch house—she needs more room anyway. Of course, we have to introduce her cat to Peetie, and that will be some drama. Maybe. Peetie likes cats."

Ray only gave him a look and returned to getting the mesquite burning.

Lucy and Grace argued about something as they lugged the coolers through the Jones's back door, making for the kitchen. The argument was good-natured, the sisters bantering as always. Lucy seemed better than she had when she'd first come home, though she was still dejected.

"Speaking of bad breakups ..." Kyle nodded at Lucy. "I seriously want to kick that guy's ass."

"You and me both." Ray and Kyle exchanged glances, bonding in their role as protective brothers.

Lucy dropped her end of the heavy cooler. She started to growl, but Hal Jenkins rushed up to the porch and caught the handle for her. Lucy stared at him in bewilderment, though Grace sent him a grateful nod.

"Hope we don't have to kick *Jenkins's* ass," Ray said darkly.

"I know." Kyle chuckled. "He could take us both out."

He and Ray watched as Hal gave Lucy a weak smile and followed Grace into the house.

"Anna wants to give Lucy a job at her vet's office," Kyle said. "As her new assistant, when Janette takes off for college."

Ray considered this. "Well, Lucy ran that big office in Houston. Or whatever it was she did there."

Kyle grinned. "I have no idea. Let's not tell her that, okay?"

Ray relaxed into one of his big laughs. "Deal."

Lucy glanced their way, frowned, and ducked inside the house.

Anna came out of it and made her way to Kyle. Kyle turned gladly to slide his arm around her waist.

"Hey, darlin'." He leaned to kiss her, liking that she lifted her face to his, readily kissing him back. No bashfulness, even though Ray stood a foot away.

"Hey, yourself," she said with a smile.

They regarded each other, Anna's blue eyes soft and full of love. Ray, with an uncharacteristic display of tact, mumbled something about bringing up another load of wood.

The breeze and smoke swirled around them as Ray went. Anna wore a windbreaker today, the October air touched with coolness. She rested light fingers on Kyle's chest.

"You know what's in one of Grace's coolers?" Anna's smile went sly. "Ice cream. And chocolate syrup."

Kyle stilled, his interest caught. "Yeah? Maybe we should try to snag us some."

"I thought of that." Anna reached into her jacket and pulled out a dark bottle.

Kyle laughed. "Oh, man. I love you."

"I love *you*." The way Anna's voice went soft dissolved everything tight inside Kyle. She was what he needed, what he'd been looking for all this time.

"If everyone's here," Kyle said. "No one will be at my place."

Even Margaret had knocked off work to attend the fundraiser. Most of Riverbend had.

Karen arrived, no Deke in sight. Interesting. She slid off the back of Jack Hillman's motorcycle and adjusted her stylish leather jacket. Even more interesting.

Tina was there, chattering with Callie and Manny Judd— she loved working at the rehab ranch, loved the horses. With luck, she'd figure out that there was more to life than chasing rodeo guys who only saw her as a brief diversion.

Right now, Tina sauntered determinedly after Deputy

Harrison, who kept a nervous eye on her while trying to watch Manny and Tracy, who were holding hands.

Mrs. Kaye waved at them, her mouth moving as she talked to the clump of people who listened politely. She gave Anna a thumbs-up, and Anna chuckled.

"She's the best," Anna said.

"Means your place is quiet too."

Anna tapped her cheek with the bottle of chocolate. "We could go back to my house, and *then* your house."

Kyle's heart beat fast and hard. "Could do that. Could do that."

"Or we could stay and have barbecue."

The sparkle in Anna's eyes told Kyle exactly what she wanted. He plucked the bottle out of her hands, cupped her cheek, and gave her a long, slow kiss.

"I say we skip dinner and go right to dessert," he said softly.

A clanging interrupted them. Callie stood on the porch, ringing an old-fashioned triangle hanging from a rafter. Heads turned, and she held up her hands. Her clear voice floated out as she stood by Ross's side, welcoming the guests and also Drew and Erica, Ray now next to her, to Riverbend.

Anna touched Kyle's lips. "We'd better go while no one's looking."

Kyle knew she was right. All eyes were on Drew, who looked abashed, and Erica, who reveled in the attention. They watched Ray as well, wondering how he and Drew would end up.

Anna seized Kyle's hand. Together they dashed from the barbecue pits, heading away from the house toward Anna's truck.

Happiness spiked high as he ran, Anna's soft hand in his,

her laughter streaming to him. He looked forward to bathing her in chocolate, licking it from her body, being welcomed into her as they sought each other in love.

Only Karen saw them go. She lifted a bottle of beer in their direction, tucked her hand more firmly under Jack's leather-jacketed arm, and smiled.

Excerpt: Ray

RIDING HARD, BOOK 7

The cowboy was muscular, solid, and stepped right in her way. Drew Paresky never saw him over the pile of paint buckets, drywall joint compound, and aluminum duct tubing half sliding out of her arms.

She ran smack into him.

The aluminum made a hell of a lot of noise as it clattered to the floor of the hardware store. The drywall joint compound followed, the bag splitting, white powder bursting out to coat Drew's jeans, the floor, and the entire front of the cowboy, whose firm body was like a wall.

"Damn it," Drew whispered as she scrambled for the things, dropping more in the process. "Damn it. *Damn* it."

Mr. Fuller, the owner of the store, popped out of another aisle and viewed the mess with dismay. He'd kick her out, and then Drew would have to figure out where else to find the mountain of things she needed.

Two large hands righted the broken bag of compound and set it against a shelf and then reached for the tubing.

"Careful now." A voice as large as the rest of him came out of the cowboy.

Drew risked a glance at his face, her own hotter than fire, and her breath deserted her.

If she had to run into someone, why did it have to be the best-looking man she'd ever seen in her life? He had dark hair under a black cowboy hat, a hard face softened by a few lines about his mouth, and wide shoulders with a sliver of chest showing above his once-black and now powder-coated shirt.

His eyes arrested her most of all. They were green, shade of jade, which sparkled in contrast to his dark hair and tanned skin.

Drew must have spent a full minute staring at his eyes. Not that she wasn't aware of the rest of his body—as rock-hard and well-formed as an artist's sculpture.

"Sorry." Drew realized she needed to say something. "Didn't see you. You okay?"

She pulled her gaze down his chest to the huge splotch of white powder that started at his chest and fully dusted his jeans.

"Damage isn't permanent," the cowboy said. "Let me help you with that. Hey, Craig—you got a cart or a trolley or something back there?"

Drew heard someone crashing around, and then a man not many years younger than the cowboy came around the corner with a flat dolly. The young man was Craig Fuller, son of the owner, who'd helped her find the right pipes and pointed her to the drywall section not ten minutes ago.

"Sorry about that. Should have given you this earlier." Craig joined the cowboy in loading all Drew's things onto the dolly. He looked critically at the remains of the bag of powder. "I'll get you some more joint compound."

Drew's defenses softened. She was a total stranger here, and had heard that small-town residents, especially in rural Texas, shut strangers out. But these two were gallantly picking up her things, helping her without a word.

"I'll pay for the broken bag," she said quickly.

"No, I will," the cowboy said. "I ran into you."

Drew shook her head. "I ran into *you*."

"Well, we can debate about that for a while, but I'll win, so don't bother." The cowboy took a card out of his wallet and passed it to Mr. Fuller. "Add it to my order," he said to the owner.

Mr. Fuller didn't give Drew time to debate. He took the cowboy's credit card and moved to the register at the front. Craig headed there too, hefting the new bag of compound to show her it was waiting for her.

"What you need all this stuff for anyway?" the cowboy asked. "Looks like you're repairing walls, plumbing, *and* electricity." He turned over the coils of wire and switch boxes, as well as wire strippers and pliers. "Someone give you a shack to fix up?"

"Sort of." Drew took a breath, tamping down her irritation, her anger, her near despair.

Before she could finish, Craig called down the aisle. "The old Paresky house. This here's Drew, Paresky's grand-daughter."

The cowboy's eyes flickered with interest. "Really? The Paresky … uh .. place?"

Drew's eyes narrowed. "You were going to say *dump*, weren't you?"

The cowboy's cheeks reddened. "Well …"

"Don't worry." Drew let out a sigh. "It is a dump. But it's my dump now."

The cowboy nodded as he looked Drew up and down with a gaze that would be considered rude—even homicidally so—in Chicago. But here, everyone stared at Drew like this. She was new, an oddity, and yet, she had roots in Riverbend.

On the other hand, she'd never been to Riverbend. Her parents hadn't brought her here on their very few visits, and while Drew had been curious about her grandparents' small town, in a vague way, her life hadn't given her time to think deeply about it.

She'd found what was known as the Hill Country and Riverbend itself to be beautiful. Refreshing. Calm. But she was already getting tired of being an object of curiosity.

"Thanks so much for helping," Drew said to end the conversation. "And sorry I ran into you."

She grabbed the handle of the dolly, trying to plow it around the cowboy and back toward the register. The wheels stuck and went every which way, explaining the clattering she'd heard before.

The cowboy grasped the bar, brushing her hands with his warm ones. A flare of heat shot through Drew, one she quickly suppressed, but her heart hammered.

He expertly maneuvered the dolly along the aisle, turned it in the open space at the end, and pushed it to the register. "There's a trick to them," he said when she caught up.

Drew took out her credit card—which would max out very soon—and used it to pay for the rest of the supplies. She winced when she saw the total.

The cowboy noticed. He stood close to her, leaning on the dolly as Craig set the purchases on it after his father rang them up. The cowboy's gaze stayed on Drew's face as she slid the card back into her wallet.

Without a word, the cowboy pushed the dolly outside for her and around the corner to the dirt lot where the customers parked for the feed store. He went directly to her small car, probably figuring from the process of elimination which was hers. Of course, it was the only *car* in the lot—all the other vehicles were pickups.

"No way you're getting all this stuff in your bitty car," the cowboy said, rightly so. "How about I haul it in my truck?" He gestured to the big black Ford 250 parked near the hay barn in the back. "I know where the Paresky place is—Out on Ranch Road 2889, right?"

"Yes." Drew swallowed. "But I can't let you ... I mean, it's nice, but I don't even know you."

One thing to have a handsome stranger help her in the store, another to have him follow her to her house. Or precede her. Drew still wasn't sure of her way around.

"I'm Ray." The cowboy stuck out his hand for her to shake. "Ray Malory. Everyone knows me."

She took his hand, finding his grip hard, fingers strong, his touch fanning the flare she tried to suppress.

"Drew," she managed, withdrawing with difficulty. "Oh, right, you already know that."

"How do you do?" The twinkle in his eyes told her the formality amused him. "Only makes sense—my truck's plenty big enough for all this. I'll meet you out there and unload it for you, then I'll leave you be. All right?"

What could she say but, "Sure." Turn down help when she needed it? A large vehicle that easily held what would take hers three trips to haul?

If he turned out to be an ax murderer, she could always

lock the door and call the cops … if the locks on the doors actually worked today and she could get her cell phone to find a signal.

Better idea—she'd get there before him and instruct him to leave everything in the driveway and go. Drew could barricade his way to the house and her daughter inside it.

The trouble was, Ray took off before Drew could get into her car and start it. He knew exactly where the old bed & breakfast lay in its derelict heap, and headed there without hesitation.

She caught up to his pickup after he'd turned from the street that led from the feed store out of town onto the road to the B&B. On maps this wider road was marked as the 2889, sometimes labeled as FM—Farm to Market, sometimes RR—Ranch Road. The name changed every mile and a half for no reason Drew could discern.

Drew caught up to Ray only because he slowed to wait for her. The posted speed was fifty, and when Drew reached Ray, he was creaking along at about thirty. When she waved at him from behind, he sped up again, taking off in a roar.

Drew's car was a small Toyota sedan that had seen better days. Not bad for driving around—and parking in—a city like Chicago and its burbs, but it was out of place in this vast land of endless and very straight roads.

Only one other vehicle passed them—another pickup—going the other way, west into town. The driver lifted a hand to Ray, and Ray waved back.

Did they know each other? Or being courteous?

Was she kidding? Everyone knew everybody in Riverbend, at least it seemed so. She was the only incongruity, the new and intriguing fixture they stared at. As out of place as her car.

Ray slowed and pulled onto the dirt road that led between fence posts—no fence or gate—to the B&B. He didn't signal, probably figuring she knew where he was going. Or maybe he never bothered to. Anyone following him in this town would already know exactly where he headed.

The lane led between two green hills that sloped down to a wide meadow. The land was deep green now, but Mrs. Ward, the lady who owned the diner, had told her that in spring, the hills would be purple with bluebonnets.

The B&B was a long two-story house situated in the curve of a drive. Trees lined the house's west side, giving it shade in the heat of the day, but the rest of the windows were open to the view—a beautiful one—of gentle hills and vast sky. The road lay hidden behind the folds of land, giving the whole place the illusion of isolated splendor.

Ray halted the truck at the end of the house near the garage—a two-story standalone building with rooms upstairs. Thank heavens for those rooms, which was where her grandfather had been living. They were the only ones habitable.

The water and electricity had been disconnected when Drew had arrived, and it had taken her a long time of arguing and producing deeds to the property before the county's electric company would turn the power back on. They were surprised she hadn't wanted to use the generator. For water, the property had a well and a pump, which Drew hadn't understood how to work. A sullen man from the county had to come out and show her. In Chicago, you paid a bill and someone you never saw flipped a switch.

Drew jumped out of the car as Ray hauled down the tailgate of his truck. Instead of unloading, he leaned on the truck bed, wiped a bead of sweat from his face, and studied the main house.

Drew's heart sank as she looked it over with him. The porch sagged, the steps to it half gone. Windows were broken and boarded up, or had simply been left gaping. The screen door was long gone—she'd found it in the grass in the back. The front door was scarred and didn't close all the way.

That was nothing to the peeling paint, fallen gutters, missing shutters, and electric wires hanging like spaghetti—thankfully hooked up only to the generator that was shut down, out of fuel.

Inside was fading or moldy wallpaper—wherever it was still on the walls—rusty plumbing fixtures, outdated and non-working appliances, rotted floors, window air conditioners that hadn't worked since 1972, and unstable ceilings.

"I think it's going to take a little more than drywall compound to fix this place up," Ray said in a slow drawl.

"No kidding. That's for repairing the apartment so my daughter and I can sleep better." Drew waved at the main house. "As you can see, you're right. A total dump."

Ray said nothing for a long time, then he left the truck and walked to the main house, stopping shy of the porch and gazing up at it, hands at his sides.

Drew joined him. "It doesn't look any better from here."

Ray glanced down at her, his green eyes unreadable. "You really going to reopen it?"

"I don't have a choice." She put her hands on her hips. "I mean, I do, but I don't. My grandfather left it to me, but only if I can fix up the B&B and make it pay within a year. If I don't …" Drew made a slicing motion with the side of her hand. "I get nothing. Not the large amount of money waiting for me after that, no property, and I'd still have to pay all the taxes before it gets gifted to a developer, as per the will. And yes, I quit my job to come out here to maybe give my daughter a better life and live on property that has been in my family for generations. *How hard could it be?* I asked myself. And here I am." She regarded the house in growing anger. "I don't know a damn thing about renovating houses, and I don't have the money to hire someone to do it for me. And I don't know why I'm spilling this to you, a total stranger."

Maybe because he stood in companionable silence, letting her talk without judgment.

"Not a *total* stranger. You did dump drywall compound all over me."

Drew laughed, with the edge of hysteria. "I am so, so sorry."

Ray shrugged, powerful shoulders moving. "I live on a ranch with cows and horses. What do you think *they* dump on me? Not to mention my little brother."

A man with cows and horses and a younger brother sounded more normal and human and real.

Not that Ray Malory was fake in any way. He had a presence that had made the Fullers, father and son, fade against him. He'd taken over, loaded her stuff, led the way out, and now looked over the house as though he knew exactly what he'd do with it.

"Mom?" The door above the garage banged open, and a girl with colt-like limbs charged down the outside stairs. "Who's this?"

She didn't ask the question in timidity, fear, or with any caution. Not Erica. She was a tough kid from the city—at least, that was how she saw herself.

"This is Ray Malory," Drew said quickly. "From River-bend. He helped me bring the supplies from the hardware store."

"Oh, sure, you went shopping and came back with a *guy*." Erica grinned. "Hi, I'm Erica," she said to Ray. "You single?"

"Erica!" Drew turned to Ray in mortification. "I'm sorry. I found her on my doorstep one day and made the mistake of feeding her."

Erica chortled. "That would be funny if I didn't look just like you."

"It's okay." Ray, fortunately, looked amused. "I am single, as it happens. So's my brother. But I think he has a crush on the vet."

"The vet?" Erica widened her eyes. "As in veterinarian? Girl vet or boy vet? Is your brother gay?" She asked in avid curiosity, no condemnation.

Ray's mouth twitched. "Dr. Anna is a lady. If my brother is gay, he hasn't told me."

"That would be cool if he was gay."

Ray rubbed his lower lip. "He might be. I'll ask him."

Drew cut off the conversation before it spun out of control. "Erica, did you finish sanding those cupboards?"

"Yep. Smooth as a baby's bottom. Not that I've ever touched one. Gross. Have you been inside our wreck?" Erica stopped next to Ray and waved at the house. "It's a pile of crap. And this town is nothings-ville in the middle of nowhere. It doesn't even have a *mall*. I mean, where do you shop?"

Drew quivered in embarrassment. "Apologize, Erica. You don't move into someone's hometown and criticize it. There are malls in Austin. We saw them on the way through, remember?"

"Yeah, but that's so far *away*. Sorry, Ray. I bet you love this place. Riverbend. All five square feet of it."

"I do love it." Ray spoke without self-consciousness. "But it takes some getting used to. I grew up here, so I know everything about it, good and bad." He looked down at Erica, at his ease. "We don't have malls because they'd go out of business, but we have the best pies on the planet at Mrs. Ward's, and most people in Riverbend have got your back."

Erica listened, actually listened, and even looked thoughtful. "Well, maybe I'll give it some more time. I doubt we'll stay long. Mom won't be able to save this place, and we'll go back home."

She spoke with conviction. Erica hadn't wanted to come, and Drew didn't blame her. Erica had friends, connections, a life back in Chicago. But she'd also had to dodge gang kids and drug dealers right on the school grounds. Not that small towns didn't have drug problems—they did, more than people knew—but Drew had decided she didn't want Erica being threatened anymore.

Before Drew could answer, the peace of the late afternoon was shattered by a long, drawn-out scream.

Drew whipped her head around to stare at the house. Shadows were lengthening, the September day starting to die. The cry came from inside the derelict house, like a shriek from an unholy creature caught in hell.

Also by Jennifer Ashley

Riding Hard

(Contemporary Romance)

Adam

Grant

Carter

Tyler

Ross

Kyle

Ray

Snowbound in Starlight Bend

Shifters Unbound

Pride Mates

Primal Bonds

Bodyguard

Wild Cat

Hard Mated

Mate Claimed

"Perfect Mate" (novella)

Lone Wolf

(In print in *Shifter Mates*)

Tiger Magic

Feral Heat

(In print in *Shifter Mates*)

Wild Wolf

Bear Attraction

Mate Bond

Lion Eyes

Bad Wolf

Wild Things

White Tiger

Guardian's Mate

Red Wolf

Midnight Wolf

Tiger Striped

A Shifter Christmas Carol

Shifter Made ("Prequel" short story)

Historical Romances

The Mackenzies Series

The Madness of Lord Ian Mackenzie

Lady Isabella's Scandalous Marriage

The Many Sins of Lord Cameron

The Duke's Perfect Wife

A Mackenzie Family Christmas: The Perfect Gift

The Seduction of Elliot McBride

The Untamed Mackenzie

(In print in *The Scandalous Mackenzies*)

The Wicked Deeds of Daniel Mackenzie

Scandal and the Duchess

(In print in *The Scandalous Mackenzies*)

Rules for a Proper Governess

The Stolen Mackenzie Bride

A Mackenzie Clan Gathering

(In print in *A Mackenzie Clan Christmas*)

Alec Mackenzie's Art of Seduction

The Devilish Lord Will

A Rogue Meets a Scandalous Lady

A Mackenzie Yuletide

(In print in *A Mackenzie Clan Christmas*)

Stormwalker

(w/a Allyson James)

Stormwalker

Firewalker

Shadow Walker

"Double Hexed"

Nightwalker

Dreamwalker

Dragon Bites

About the Author

New York Times bestselling and award-winning author Jennifer Ashley has written more than 100 published novels and novellas in romance, urban fantasy, mystery, and historical fiction under the names Jennifer Ashley, Allyson James, and Ashley Gardner. Jennifer's books have been translated into more than a dozen languages and have earned starred reviews in *Publisher's Weekly* and *Booklist*. When she isn't writing, Jennifer enjoys playing music (guitar, piano, flute), reading, hiking, and building dollhouse miniatures.

More about Jennifer's books can be found at
http://www.jenniferashley.com

To keep up to date on her new releases, join her newsletter here:
http://eepurl.com/47kLL

Made in the USA
Monee, IL
26 July 2022